MW01123197

THE GROVER SCHOOL PLEDGE

THE
GROVER
SCHOOL
PLEDGE

WANDA TAYLOR

Illustrations by Nneka Myers

HarperCollins*Publishers*Ltd

Published by HarperCollins Publishers Ltd

First edition

HarperCollins Publishers Ltd
Bay Adelaide Centre, East Tower
22 Adelaide Street West, 41st Floor
Toronto, Ontario, Canada
M5H 4E3

www.harpercollins.ca

Library and Archives Canada Cataloguing in Publication

Title: The Grover School pledge / Wanda Taylor.
Names: Taylor, Wanda Lauren, author.
Identifiers: Canadiana (print) 20220470189 | Canadiana (ebook)
20220470197 | ISBN 9781443467254 (hardcover) |
ISBN 9781443467261 (EPUB)
Subjects: LCGFT: Fiction.
Classification: LCC PS8639.A97 G76 2023 | DDC jC813/.6—dc23

Printed and bound in the United States of America
23 24 25 26 27 LBC 5 4 3 2 1

*For the real Arlaina and all those who have an uncommon name.
It may not be found written on a pencil or a key chain, but
it is beautiful and unique and special, just like you.*

*Also for Sara, Devon, Cory and Kayleigh—
my other loyal supporters.*

*And for little Aaniya, Arielle and Kendall, who always
let me know when I was getting it right.*

Chapter 1

Who Am I?

"Arlaina!"

Mom's voice drills through my ears just as I am getting ready to say goodbye to Tina and hang up the cordless phone. Even on the other line, Tina can hear my mom calling from the living room downstairs.

"Coming!" I sit up on the edge of the bed and slide both feet into my fuzzy purple slippers.

"What does your mom want?" Tina asks.

"She's going to put my hair into braids before bed." I pull my hand through thick, black curls. My index finger gets stuck in a tangle.

"I wish I could have braids," Tina says.

I hop from my bed toward the phone base on the nightstand. "You can't have braids," I joke. Tina doesn't laugh.

"Why can't I have braids?"

"They might look a little silly in your straight, blond hair. Maybe one weekend we can braid it and see. Anyway, I have to go. Mom's gonna yell back up here again."

"Okay. Can't wait to hear your oral presentation tomorrow."

"Can't wait to hear yours."

I hang up the phone and rush downstairs. When I walk into the living room, Mom is standing behind a chair that she's pulled from the kitchen, her shiny, black afro wrapped in the yellow headscarf she sleeps in. She taps the back of the chair for me to come and sit. The hair oil and moisturizer are laid out on the coffee table beside her.

"Not just any braids, Mom. I want a pattern in my parts, okay?" I leap into the chair. "I need to look good for my presentation tomorrow."

"Those patterns will be fifty dollars extra." Mom grins.

"Okay, take it out of my allowance."

Mom takes the blue comb with the skinny teeth and starts parting my hair.

"Nervous?" she whispers.

"Yes."

"Don't worry, honey. Isn't the topic of your presentation Who Am I? That's a great chance for you to share some of your culture with a room full of friends. Think of it like that."

"Thanks. I will."

My nerves start to settle as Mom goes to work on my hair. After about an hour, she is finally finished. Like always,

I rush over to the flower-shaped mirror on the wall as soon as the last piece of hair is braided.

"It looks good, Mom." I smile at my image in the mirror.

"Of course it does. Now you can go upstairs and get ready for bed. I'll see you in the morning."

I walk into Mr. Matthews' class with Tina. We are both nervous about our presentations, but we aren't the only ones. Everyone looks scared. Tina compliments my hair for the third time as we head to our seats. It's getting close to summer vacation, and I can't wait to have a break from Mr. Matthews. He always reminds us that he's been a teacher at Grover Public School since it opened. That means he's really old. The school was built back when Mississauga started growing a lot around Central Parkway. And it's still growing fast. Even though my family has been living in the area for a long time, every year it seems to be changing more and more. The families moving in. The buildings going up. Just this week I've been watching a Black family do renovations inside an abandoned store. Yesterday I watched a man drill a sign over its door that read *Kendall's Shop* and I got excited. I hope they sell Black hair products in this new store. Then we won't have to drive halfway across the city to get them anymore.

The changes to our neighbourhood are good. As more people from different backgrounds move here, the area feels way more lively. The city put up a new playground at the end of our street. I feel like I'm too old to actually play on it, but sometimes me and Tina will hop on a swing and talk about important stuff, like boys and why our parents won't let us have cell phones yet. When we leave Grover, we'll be going into middle school. We need to have cell phones, or we'll be grade seven losers.

Two weeks ago, when Mr. Matthews asked us to write an autobiographical sketch of ourselves and present it to the class, everybody was annoyed. I remember Tina complaining the loudest.

"Seriously? Do we really have to do this audio-biographical?" She was slouched over in her chair with her elbows planted on the desk, like always, and her face resting in her hands. Mr. Matthews pushed his red-rimmed glasses up on his nose and squished his face.

"It's called an auto . . . bio . . . graphical . . . sketch, Tina. It's all about you. And I don't know why this class is groaning. This is an assignment you would have normally done at the beginning of the school year, anyway."

"This sucks," Tina told him.

Mr. Matthews explained that waiting until near the end of the year gives us a chance to think about who we are as we enter middle school.

I blend in with the other nervous students now piling into class and pulling their oral reports from their bags. Tina slides in to her desk. I slide in to mine next to her. My hands shake a little as I grab my presentation out of my bag.

"Okay, settle in, boys and girls." Mr. Matthews waves his hands for quiet. He pushes his glasses up his nose and plops into his wheely chair. He lets it swivel.

"Who wants to present first?"

No one answers.

"This should be an easy assignment for you, Arlaina, since you like to talk about yourself so much. Do you want to go first?"

A few of the boys laugh. Mr. Matthews seems amused by his ridiculous joke.

"No thanks." I swat my hand as if I'm batting at a fly. I don't want the class to know I'm bothered by what Mr. Matthews says, so I pretend not to care. If I was bold enough, I would say something rude back to him, but I don't really know what to say.

A few other kids raise their hands to go first, and I am relieved. During the presentations, I learn that Preet and her family are new immigrants to Canada, and that Mitchell was adopted from an orphanage. I definitely didn't know that Tina's grandmother used to be the Mississauga mayor. I had to hear it from her presentation. We've been best friends since kindergarten. She should have told me something big like that a long time ago.

Halfway through the presentations, Mr. Matthews calls my name to go next. I take in a deep breath, scoop my paper in my hands and head to the front of the class. I had Mom read it over last night to make sure I didn't forget anything. She told me to include some Black history. She thinks some schools do a bad job of teaching kids about that. Most of what I know about it comes from what my family told me. I don't remember ever hearing Mr. Matthews talk about Black history.

Standing in front of the room, I look out over the faces that I've been seeing every day for a whole school year. I know I'll probably never see some of them again once summer vacation starts. I'm unhappy about that, but I hope we'll see each other out at the malls sometime.

"The title of my autobiographical sketch is 'Who Is Arlaina Jefferson?'" I shift my feet and squeeze the report between my sweaty, brown fingers. "It wasn't that long ago when my grandfather, Clyde—he's dead now—told me that every life is very precious."

"Please, speak up, Arlaina. Everyone needs to hear you." Mr. Matthews' long, awkward body is folded down into his chair. He leans sideways toward me when he speaks, causing his chair to tip. He slams his foot on the floor and grabs onto the desk to try and catch his balance. I laugh out loud by mistake. Mr. Matthews looks annoyed. A few of the students giggle too. Mr. Matthews gives me a death look.

"Continue, Arlaina," he growls. I'm used to Mr. Matthews' grumbling. Maybe he thinks it makes him scarier. I look over at him when I read my next sentence.

"My grandfather taught me that it is most important to have a heart filled with love for others." Mr. Matthews folds his arms, but I think he's listening to the words.

"He said it's because we can never know when something or someone will be gone. And I thought about that while I was writing this essay. My grandfather died during a protest march. He was born in America in the fifties, and there was a lot of racism. Black people were not wanted and were not allowed in certain places, like restaurants and movie theatres. But my grandfather still had love for everyone. He still forgave, for all the pain he suffered."

I look up from the paper to take a pause. When I lift my eyebrows, I feel the tightness of those freshly laid braids. I push a few of the long, dangling ones back behind my shoulder. I feel weird talking about racism because my grandfather's experiences sound so horrible. But I also feel proud that he fought so others could be treated like equals. I hope he is looking down and feeling proud of me for speaking about it. I smile to myself.

"Now, my name is not one you hear every day. It is my grandmother's middle name. She was a secretary for one of the most powerful Black organizations. Everybody knew her because she helped so many Black people get jobs and get an education." I take another deep breath. When I look up this time, everyone seems to be paying attention. This makes me feel confident. I keep reading.

"My mother, Anita, has a huge herb and vegetable garden in our backyard. Every year at harvest, she takes all the vegetables to the local church to be given out to families who can't afford fresh vegetables. I get to help her with the harvest and give it out on church harvest day. My dad,

Gregory, is a woodworker who makes furniture, and my mother runs a flower shop."

A boy sitting directly in front of me suddenly starts twisting his report around a chewed-up pencil. I want him to stop. His fidgeting is distracting me, and I just want to get the presentation finished. Maybe he is scared because he hasn't had his turn yet. I try to ignore him and keep reading.

"My brother, Kyle, is thirteen. He's two years older than me, but most of the time, Kyle acts much younger. Before summer is over, he'll be fourteen and I'll be twelve. Then I'll have to put up with him not just at home but in the same middle school." This gets some laughs from the class, maybe because the boys tease their sisters too. I chuckle and relax. I'm glad Mom's idea to add in some funny parts is working.

When my presentation is finally over, I feel happy. I sit back down but I can hardly pay attention to what the others are saying after me. I keep playing over in my head the parts of my presentation that got the laughs. I feel really good that everybody was listening when I talked about my grandfather. I want to be bold like him someday.

I am still in the clouds when me and Tina walk home after school. She is feeling excited about her presentation too.

"Let's go to the swings." She smiles. We start jogging along the sidewalk. Tina's long ponytail flops up and down. My braids swish from side to side. We plan to have a good chat on the swings.

Just then, one of the boys from our class comes running past us.

"Hey, Oreo cookies! Better walk faster, it's gonna rain."

Tina looks at me and her face softens. "Don't worry about him, Arlaina, he's rude. Always looking for attention."

"You know what he meant, though, don't you?" I ask.

"Yeah."

"Because you're white and I'm . . ."

"I said yeah. But who cares?"

I do notice how I'm looked at differently from Tina sometimes, like one Saturday when we were at the beach. Two blond girls came over to us and asked Tina if she wanted to swim out to the big rock with them, and they didn't ask me. Tina didn't go because she was sunburned. But she couldn't see why it bothered me. I don't think she gets it.

"Don't you think that's why Mr. Matthews always makes comments to me too?"

"No. I think Mr. Matthews is just a goof with big ugly glasses."

We keep walking. I don't say anything else about it, but I feel a little weird. I try to stop thinking about it. Tina asks for a race, and we sprint all the way home.

CHAPTER 2

The New Arrival

The last class of the day seems long, and I don't plan to hang around when the dismissal bell rings. The presentations yesterday gave me a good feeling. The Oreo cookie comment did not. But today, my cousin Patrice and her family are coming by my house right after school with an exciting gift. They are moving to New York when school closes for the summer. My uncle is a shipbuilder, and his company is relocating. I'll be so sad to see Patrice go, but she is leaving her pet rabbit with me, since she can't take any animals with her. They have to go to Nova Scotia for two weeks first, because my uncle has two weeks of training at the Halifax Shipyard before they drive to New York. I will be rushing home so I can get there before they do. It's so exciting!

Patrice named her rabbit Obeena. She says it means destiny and courage. Mom said Patrice probably made that up. I think it's a fun name to say out loud. And we both have names that are different. I like that. I stare up at the apple-shaped clock above the chalkboard, then I lean over to Tina's desk.

"As soon as the bell rings, I'm dipping," I whisper.

"Oh yeah, Patrice's rabbit comes today. Did you and your mom get the rabbit food?" she whispers back.

"We went yesterday. We even got extra shavings and rabbit treats and everything." My face is beaming. Mr. Matthews catches us chatting and stops teaching.

"Excuse me, Miss Jefferson, would you like to share your thoughts with the whole class?"

"Um . . . no." Some students snicker. The back of my neck starts to feel hot. So do my cheeks. Luckily, my brown skin never turns red, but it still feels bad.

"I suggest you pay attention, Arlaina. It's disrespectful."

"Sorry, Mr. Matthews." I notice he doesn't say anything to Tina.

I fold my arms and start thinking of all the ways I could get back at Mr. Matthews in a big way. Maybe I'll crush his glasses or put crazy glue on his chair. But those things don't feel big enough. Mr. Matthews needs to learn a lesson about being mean to me. I stare at the hands on the clock again. They move in slow motion. I quietly tap my fingers to the rhythm of the skinny hand ticking around, second by second. Now I can't look away. The tiny hand beats on. One second. Two seconds. Three seconds. I can't think of something I could do about Mr. Matthews, so instead I try to think of a hip-hop song that matches the rhythm of the clock in my head.

As soon as one comes to me, I play the chorus on repeat over and over in my head. I don't know the verses, just the melody. But it's all I need for a distraction. After what seems like forever, the bell finally rings. It startles me. Mr. Matthews keeps speaking. I toss my work into my book bag and jump out of my seat. I don't even notice that the other students are still sitting as I'm heading toward the door.

"Not so fast, Miss Jefferson. What's your hurry?" Mr. Matthews calls me out in front of the class. Everyone else sits stiff, like they're afraid to move unless Mr. Matthews says they can. But I'm in a hurry today. I stretch my arms out and shrug my shoulders. "Didn't the bell ring?"

Mr. Matthews rubs his chalky hands through his hair.

"Yes, but I'm still talking." He points to my desk. The sweat stains on his yellow shirt are showing. His fuzzy brown hair has patches of chalk in it from rubbing his head every time someone does something he doesn't like. I stomp back to my seat. After Mr. Matthews is finished rambling, he finally lets us go. On my way out, he stops me.

"I really have to go, Mr. Matthews. My cousin is bringing her rabbit over to my house today and I need to get home fast."

"Oh, a rabbit?"

I roll my eyes to the ceiling and sigh. I know he's about to be nosy.

"Yes. They're moving to New York soon and I'm adopting her rabbit," I quickly spill. I just want to get going.

"New York? Well, I have a sister in New York. That's a really busy place to raise a family." He puts his hands on his skinny hips. I wonder if he can tell that I don't care. His sister has nothing to do with me and my life. I start walking away.

"And a rabbit is not an easy pet to look after either, Arlaina. I hope you know rabbits require a lot of care. I sure hope you're prepared to take on that kind of responsibility."

I sure hope he eats my dust as I sprint away from his classroom. Without answering him back, I zip down the hall and burst out the front doors. Tina catches up to me halfway down the block.

"Wait up! Gee, you didn't even wait for me. Why?" Tina is panting, out of breath.

"I didn't want to jinx it," I answer.

Tina pulls her hair back into the loose ponytail it keeps falling out of.

"Hey! I'm no jinx!" she says. "If you're going to have a rabbit, I'm going to be there all the time to help you, right?"

"I didn't mean it like that. I just don't need everyone telling me what to do." I pull my book bag over my shoulder.

"I know. I heard Mr. Matthews talking to you. Do you think he's right, that it will be a lot of work?"

"See? This is what I mean," I mutter.

"Sorry." Tina pats my shoulder. "I want to come over and see the rabbit too."

13

"You're not gonna try and follow behind Jonathan on the way home today, are you?"

"No. I really want to come and see the rabbit."

"Okay, I guess so then."

Tina has a crush on a boy at school named Jonathan, but he pays no attention to her. Sometimes she tries to drag me with her while she trails behind him after school. It's very annoying. Even I can see that to Jonathan she's invisible. Tina follows me the rest of the way to my house. There's no Jonathan in sight. Tina and I sing choruses from Kidz Bop, those kids who sing famous people's songs and make albums out of them. We dance down the sidewalk as if we're Kidz Bop artists performing for the cars whizzing by. We're both super excited for the new arrival.

CHAPTER 3

The Sad Goodbye

As soon as Tina and I turn onto our street, I see Patrice's car parked behind Dad's.

"Oh no! They're already here!" I start rushing up the driveway. Tina is close behind me. I swing the door open, and the first person I see is Patrice. We scream. Tina and I drop our bags as Patrice rushes toward me with her arms wide open. Right away, I notice Patrice is wearing a bright peach scarf wrapped around the base of her big, bushy afro. She has on a white tank top with that flower-patterned skirt my mother gave her on her birthday last year. I love that Patrice is always dressed like she's a fashion model. I want to be just like her when I'm her age.

"Little cousin!" Patrice shouts as she wraps her arms around my shoulders. I squeeze my bony arms around her waist.

"Patrice!" I squeal.

"Hi, Patrice." Tina gives Patrice an awkward wave. She thinks Patrice doesn't like her. I try to assure her all the time it isn't true. Patrice says that some white people believe they're better than Black people. Whenever she talks about that, Tina always thinks Patrice means her too, because she's white. I asked Patrice once to tell Tina that she wasn't one of those kinds of white people. But Patrice refused. Even though she knows Tina isn't one of those, she thinks Tina's mom secretly wishes she didn't have a Black best friend. I told Patrice that Tina's mom is always nice to me. But Patrice said a smile can be fake and being nice doesn't mean anything. Me and Tina don't care that we are different. We just love hanging out together. But I decided it was better not to push the issue with Patrice again. I can't help how Patrice feels and I can't help how Tina feels.

Tina says hello to Patrice a second time. Patrice gives her a half smile, then grabs me by the hand. Tina follows as Patrice pulls me through the house.

"Where's Obeena?" I ask.

"She's over here," Mom calls out.

Patrice leads me. Mom and Aunt Dottie are sitting at the dining room table, drinking hot tea. Obeena is out of the cage, hopping around on the carpet and sniffing everything in her path.

"Hey, Mom. Hey, Aunt Dottie," I sing.

"Hi, Arlaina." Aunt Dottie smiles. "Obeena has been waiting for you."

"I've been waiting for her too." I'm grinning.

I kneel in front of Obeena. She is beautiful and brown. I hope to scoop her into my arms, but she takes off in the other direction. I'm shocked and I stop grinning. Patrice notices and sits on the floor beside me. I've never owned a pet before and already I'm not good at it.

"Don't worry, Arlaina, rabbits are like that," Aunt Dottie says.

"That's how they protect themselves," Mom adds.

"So, it's not me?" I'm still worried.

"No." Patrice laughs. "She just needs to get used to you, that's all. Here, let me get her."

Patrice slowly approaches Obeena. She doesn't run into Patrice's arms, but she doesn't dash away either. Patrice sings Obeena's name. Obeena takes one hop in the other direction, then stops. The fluffy brownish-white fur on her belly moves up and down as she breathes in and out. Patrice rubs her fur. Obeena's nose wiggles and sniffs while Patrice talks softly.

"You have a new mamma, now. Arlaina will take really good care of you, okay?" It's like Obeena stops to listen to Patrice's voice and can understand what she is saying. I know rabbits can't understand humans, but it really looks like she can. Patrice picks Obeena up and cradles the rabbit in her arms. Obeena doesn't squirm, she just lies there. Patrice puts Obeena across her shoulder and strokes her fur some more.

"Come here, Arlaina. I'll show you how to hold her," Patrice says.

I slowly crawl over to where Patrice is sitting. Tina follows me, crouching down on the floor with us.

"Now, pet her fur there." Patrice shows me how.

I smooth my hand along Obeena's back. She doesn't jump. She seems to enjoy the attention.

"See? She likes that." Patrice giggles.

Tina reaches over and strokes Obeena's back too.

"Isn't that sweet?" Aunt Dottie says. She and Mom have been watching the whole time.

"I don't know about that, Dottie. Look at all the rabbit poop she's leaving behind. Are you cleaning that up?"

"Nope!" Aunt Dottie shakes her head. Mom rolls her eyes.

"Now, Arlaina, I'm going to put her across your shoulder," Patrice advises me. "You have to gently put one hand under her butt and slowly pet her with the other hand."

I'm a little nervous but I'm dying to hold her. I want her to like me. I already promised Patrice that I would take good care of her.

Patrice lays Obeena across my shoulder slowly. She moves around a bit, but she doesn't jump away from me. She grips my sweater with her claws, like she's afraid. I wonder if she can tell that I'm afraid too. I put one hand under her butt like Patrice told me to, and I start petting her with my other hand. Her fur feels so smooth between my fingers. I move them up and down to the rhythm of her breathing as I rub near her tummy. She sniffs all around my ear and my neck. The tickly feeling makes me giggle.

"I think she likes you already." Patrice smiles.

"I think so too," Tina agrees.

Just then, Dad, Kyle and Patrice's father, Gus, come in through the kitchen door.

"That'll be the boys," Mom announces. "Your father didn't seem too pleased about this new arrival. It took a lot of convincing to get him to agree to it."

"Oh, Greg is just an old fart, just like his brother Gus," Aunt Dottie jokes. They both laugh.

The tall, thin brothers stand in the entry to the dining room. Kyle peeks in from between them. "What's so funny?" Uncle Gus asks.

"We were laughing at you two," Aunt Dottie answers. "You're more alike than you know."

Dad grins, but I know he has no idea what Aunt Dottie means. She sips the last bit of her tea and gets up from the table.

"Well, Gus, we should be going. We have a lot of last-minute things to do before we get on our way," Aunt Dottie says.

"It's like a nineteen-hour drive to Nova Scotia," Mom says.

"We're flying." Aunt Dottie looks confused and squishes her face. "Did you forget? Gus's company is shipping our car down while he does his training. We're only driving from Nova Scotia to New York."

"Still." Mom is being negative.

"Don't be a worry wart," Uncle Gus tells her. "We could

fly to New York too, but we want Patrice to experience the drive instead. It's going to be a fun road trip for us."

Mom gets up from the table and hugs Aunt Dottie. Dad and Uncle Gus hug each other too. Soon, everybody's hugging, even Tina. Patrice and I can't let each other go. We are both crying. Tina stands nearby, awkwardly.

"Who's going to tell me how to match my colours? And who will tell me that my sweater looks horrible with my skirt?" I say between sniffles.

"That will still be me, little cousin. Except I just won't be down the street anymore."

Patrice sniffles too. We wipe each other's tears. Even though Patrice is fourteen, she still makes me feel important. She never looks down on me or makes me feel like I'm too young to be around her.

All the parents and Kyle head toward the front door.

"I'm going to miss hanging out with you and your friends," I say. "It's so funny listening to you guys make fun of things people say about Black people." The remembering makes me grin.

"Ha, like how we only eat fried chicken and watermelon?" Patrice laughs.

"Yeah, too funny! And I'm really going to miss all the talks about boys and makeup."

I notice Tina lowering her head. I can still talk about those things with Tina, but it's different with Patrice. She and her friends know everything.

"That's okay, we can still talk about all that stuff, if Auntie ever lets you get a cell phone." Patrice shakes her head.

"I know, right? Can you talk to her real quick before you go?" I glance over at Tina. "And tell her to talk to Tina's mom too. We both need cell phones."

Tina looks up at me and smiles. She feels included.

"Auntie will probably bite my head off. But I'll say something as we're walking out the door. That way she can't say anything back."

We head to the front door. Patrice's parents are already out on the step, waving. Mom, Dad and Kyle are in the doorway.

"Come on, Patrice. We can't say goodbye forever," Uncle Gus calls from outside.

Patrice squeezes through Mom and Dad in the doorway.

"Be good for your mom." Dad pats Patrice on the back.

"I will."

Me and Tina squeeze through Mom and Dad and watch Patrice from the step. When the three of them are in the car, Patrice rolls down the back window.

"Auntie!" she calls, waving a bony arm out the window.

"Yes?"

"Please give my cousin a cell phone! I need to check in on her."

The car rolls out of the driveway. Uncle Gus honks his horn. We stare at them until the car is out of sight. Patrice didn't mention Tina's name, and I'm not surprised. But I know that if Mom gets me a cell, Tina's mom will get her one too.

"A cell phone, huh?" Mom looks at me with a side-eye as she disappears from the doorway with Dad and Kyle. I look over at Tina; we shrug our shoulders. We're not sure if my mom's look is a yes or a no.

CHAPTER 4

My Brother, the Turd

I'm sitting cross-legged in the corner of the dining room, watching Obeena hop around. I'm not paying any attention to the time. I know I have a lot of responsibility now and I have to give Obeena all the attention I can. It's her first whole day in her new surroundings and I want to get this right.

"Now remember, you are responsible for feeding her and cleaning up after her," Mom reminds me as she passes by.

"I know. I got this, Mom."

When Mom disappears down the hall, I watch Obeena sniff at every crack and turn. She bounces all around the room. Mom wasn't too happy that she was left to clean up the rabbit turd from yesterday. I'm sure that's why she's giving me a warning. She made me promise that whenever I have Obeena out of her cage, I'll clean up any droppings she leaves behind. I just have to make sure I do that.

When I finally look up at the old wooden clock on the dining room wall, I see that it's already past five o'clock. That's time for supper. Dad walks past in the hall a few times. When he pops into the dining room, Obeena dashes across his path. He grunts and twists the corner of his mouth. Kyle comes in just as Dad is leaving. He sits next to me on the floor. At first Kyle just sits quietly and watches Obeena move around. He tips his head to the side and squishes his forehead, like he's waiting for Obeena to speak or something. After a few minutes, Kyle sighs and gets up from the floor.

"What a boring old bunny," he says.

"She is not boring," I grumble.

"Sure she is. I've been sitting here a whole five minutes and she's done nothing but hop and poop. That's totally boring," he replies.

"She's special, Kyle. Patrice said her name means destiny and courage."

Kyle grabs his stomach and bursts out laughing.

"You're rude." I cross my arms and huff.

That makes Kyle laugh even harder. He leaves the dining room, but I can still hear him laughing as he heads out the kitchen door. I am so mad at him for making fun of me and Obeena. Kyle was mean before, but now, with Obeena here, I think he's going to be an even bigger problem.

"Back in the cage, Obeena. It's time for us to eat," Mom sings out when she enters the dining room. My arms are still crossed. I look up at Mom to make sure she can see my pout.

24

"Arlaina, why are you sitting in here sulking?"

"Because Kyle is a meanie."

"What did he do now?"

"He said Obeena is boring."

Mom laughs. I don't think it's funny at all. Mom must not see how big this is for me. I hope she won't be like Kyle and think this whole thing is just a joke.

"I'm sorry for laughing, honey, I don't mean to. Bunnies hop. They sleep. They eat. They poop. That's it. That would be very boring to a thirteen-year-old boy."

"Why did you say I can have her, then, if no one even wants her around?" I groan.

"That's not true, Arlaina. I didn't say we don't want her."

"Dad doesn't. Kyle doesn't."

"I guess your father has his reasons, but she's here, isn't she?" Mom rubs my back. "And don't worry about Kyle. He's doing what brothers do. How about I take Obeena upstairs to your room while you clean up her mess. We need to get the table set in here."

Without answering, I get up to go get the hand broom from my room. It's been sitting in there since my popcorn spill a few days ago. Mom scoops Obeena and follows me up the stairs. The smell of pine and cedar shavings fills my nose when I open my bedroom door. It reminds me of the tree smells at the cabin we rent during the summer.

Mom puts Obeena in her cage and hooks the latch. I watch Obeena rush to the water bottle attached to the inside of her cage and start drinking. The tiny metal ball inside the water tube clicks faster and faster. Obeena is drinking like it's her last chance to have water. Mom notices this too.

"Do you see this, Arlaina? You kept her downstairs for too long. Just look at how thirsty she is."

"But she can't talk, so how would I know when she needs to drink?"

"This, you will learn," Mom replies. "You've got to remember that your rabbit's cage is her home, just like this house is your home. In this house, you have everything you need. Food, water, a bathroom, a place to sleep. But if you leave here for too long, you will miss your supper. Then you will start to get thirsty and hungry. When it gets dark, you'll start whining for your bed."

"No, just for my pillow," I joke. Mom twists her mouth. I know what she's trying to say, I just don't want to be wrong.

"Don't keep her away from her cage for too long, okay?"

"Yes, Mom." I smile.

"And don't even get me started about those disgusting little rabbit droppings all over the place." Mom frowns and waves a finger in the air. "Get back downstairs quickly and clean up the dining room before your father sees it."

I grab the hand broom and dustpan. I'm not happy about this chore. I think the poop is gross too. Maybe this is what Mr. Matthews was talking about when he said rabbits are a lot of work. I put Mr. Matthews' words to the back of my mind. I can't let him be right. Mom follows me back downstairs, all the while still talking about Obeena and all the turds.

"Which turd, the rabbit droppings or Kyle?" I laugh at my own joke. Mom doesn't.

"Keep it moving, missy, I'll give you ten minutes to get this done. And stop calling your brother a turd."

Mom turns to the kitchen while I step back into the dining room. I look at all the tiny turds scattered around the floor, and all I can do is frown. I think cleaning up has to be the nastiest part of owning a pet. As I'm cleaning, I think about Patrice. She made owning a rabbit sound like so much fun. Whenever I went over to her house, she seemed to be so happy with Obeena. Taking her out of her cage, feeding her and petting her. I admired her for that. She seemed so responsible.

I guess I never saw the grosser sides of it. Of course rabbits poop, but I never gave a thought about someone having to go behind them and clean it up. Or that it's messy, and that their pee really stinks. Mom is right, they eat and sleep and poop. But I promised Patrice, and I want to get better at taking care of Obeena. So, I have to be the one to take care of the clean-up too, even if it's not fun.

CHAPTER 5

Being Responsible

I'm still on my hands and knees in the dining room scooping up turds when Mom comes in to set the table. I try to stay out of her way as she lays plates and utensils in front of everyone's spots. But rabbit droppings are tiny and hard and round. Every time I get the poop onto the little dustpan, some of them roll off and back onto the floor. I'm gagging and I'm getting really annoyed.

"Arlaina, what is taking you so long?"

"They keep falling off," I whine.

"Really? Are you telling me you can't sweep this mess properly? Or are you just being lazy? Scoop some and put it in the garbage. Go back and get more, scoop that into the garbage. What's so hard about that? I will not bring any food in here until you get this done."

"I'm almost finished," I lie.

I feel panicked by Mom's impatience. I want to tell her

28

to come try it and see how hard it is, but I know that suggestion would make her mad. Dad isn't super excited about Obeena, but if Mom sees me trying, she will tell him. If I don't keep things clean, Dad might say she has to go! I keep scooping.

Mom heads back to the kitchen, and finally I get the rest of the poop onto the dustpan and carry it out to the kitchen garbage. Mom is in there scooping food from the pots into big serving dishes. It smells amazing.

"What did you make, Mom?" I go in closer to see if there's anything I can sneak into my mouth. Mom shrieks when she sees me come too close to the serving dishes.

"Hey! Get going! You haven't even washed your hands yet."

"Sorry." I take off from the kitchen fast. I know how much Mom hates it when people hang around food with dirty hands.

While I'm running water in the bathroom, I can hear Dad and Kyle in the dining room, laughing. I squeeze way too much liquid soap across my fingers and lather it up. The laughter gets louder. Then I hear Mom clanging the serving dishes down on the table. I speed up my hand washing and rush into the dining room. I don't want to miss anything.

"Hey, girl." Dad kisses my cheek when I enter the dining room. I plop down in my spot at the table just as Mom is bringing the glasses and juice pitcher in. The food on the table looks delicious. Spicy curried chicken. Black-eyed peas and rice. Sweet potato slices smothered in melted butter and brown sugar. Plantain. Homemade herb and cheese tea biscuits. I can't wait to dig in.

Dad says a quick prayer, then we all dive in to the food. No one is really talking. We are all too busy smacking our lips and licking our fingers.

"Gosh, you guys are extra hungry tonight." Mom laughs.

"Yeah. My stomach is hitting the high notes while all this good food is going down," Kyle says with a grin. As I'm eating, I'm thinking about whether I should talk to Mom and Dad about Mr. Matthews' bad attitude. They would probably think I'm exaggerating and tell me to just keep doing my schoolwork. I start to wonder if I should mention it to Kyle instead. I think I have a better chance with him than Mom and Dad. Kyle might have some idea how to help me get back at Mr. Matthews. I'll probably bring it up to him when he's not being a dork.

As I'm licking curry chicken sauce from my fingers, I notice some stray rabbit droppings near Dad's chair.

My mouth drops. I don't know how I missed them! Mom notices my face.

"Arlaina, is something wrong?"

"No," I lie.

I keep eating, hoping that Dad doesn't turn around and notice the disgusting turds behind him. If Dad drops his fork on the floor, I'm doomed. I'm so nervous. I slow down my chewing, almost like I'm afraid to move my face and body too much. Of course, Mom notices me. She doesn't miss anything.

"Goodness, Arlaina, you've stopped eating. Are you full already?"

"Probably from all the fun she had staring at that boring bunny," Kyle blurts out.

"Kyle." Mom warns him with a mean look.

"What?" Kyle pretends not to know what he's done.

"That'll be enough about the rabbit," Mom replies.

"I'm fine, Mom," I say and go back to eating so she doesn't keep asking.

"Speaking of that rabbit," Dad starts. Oh no, he sees the poop! "Gus gave Patrice's other rabbit to that grouchy lady who lives at the end of the street. You know, Edna Wilson. Maybe Edna would also be interested in taking this one." He looks right at me.

"No way, Dad." I scowl.

"Old Edna doesn't like kids, but she sure loves animals," he teases.

"Those two rabbits together would multiply like anything, wouldn't they, Dad?" Kyle shrieks.

"Yes, but that would be Edna's problem."

"Greg, I know you don't like this whole idea, but it's only been a day. Give Arlaina a chance with Obeena," Mom says.

"Dad," I plead. "I promise I can take good care of her."

"And what about your schoolwork?" Dad asks.

"School is almost over. And I have the whole summer to show you."

"Okay, well, I'm going to keep my eye on you, Arlaina. You've agreed to take on this responsibility, so if you can show me that you are able to care for a pet properly, it can stay. But if you are careless, the rabbit goes. Got it?"

I nod my head. I can't figure out why Dad is so against Obeena. She's just a little rabbit. I think he likes being difficult. But I know I have to prove this to him. I remember the random turds not far away from his chair. I guess that's not a very good start.

"Great! Now let's just finish eating. I made an amazing pineapple upside-down cake for dessert," Mom announces.

Dad's face lights up when he hears what's for dessert. It's his favourite. He would eat the whole cake by himself if Mom would let him. He rubs his hands together and shoves his empty plate away. "Well, I'm ready! Bring it on!" he says, patting his belly.

Mom hops up to go get the cake. I'm not sure what makes Dad look around his chair, but I only turn away for one second and then I hear him gasp. I whip my neck around to him.

"Oh my God. Please tell me I do not see what I think I see, in the same room where I am eating my meal." Dad slaps his hand across his forehead. Oh no, I'm caught!

Kyle follows Dad's eyes and looks in the direction of the turds sitting in a small pile near Dad's chair.

"Friggin' gross!" Kyle covers his mouth with his hand and stands in the corner of the dining room, gagging. Mom comes in with the cake. She realizes what just happened and she looks at Dad. They both look disappointed.

"Don't worry, I'll clean it up." I jump up from the table.

"Does this mean dinner is over?" Dad squishes his face in disgust and gets up from the table. "After seeing poop, I'll feel like I'm eating it."

I'm praying he doesn't say we have to give Obeena away. Kyle laughs as Dad leaves the dining room. My forehead is burning. I glare at Kyle, but there's nothing I can say.

I tried my best. I don't know if anyone gets that. I start to feel a tight knot in my stomach. I know I need to open my mouth, but I don't. Patrice never warned me about this happening, so if I did speak now, what would I even say without making things worse? This probably never happened to Patrice. She would have caught every turd. I think it's better not to say anything to her about it. I squeeze the knot in my stomach, but it doesn't help.

I pick up the turds in my hand and let them roll across my palm. In my head, I know it's gross, but I just want them to be gone. I take them out to the gar- bage and tip my hand upside down to let them fall in. I want to gag. I think this is what parents feel

like when they clean their babies' dirty diapers. Although a turd is maybe not as messy. I have to get better at the clean-up side of owning a rabbit, to make sure there's never a repeat of tonight.

CHAPTER 6

A Heap of Trouble

Mom enters the dining room and sits back down at the table. She watches me playing with my food. I know she wants to tell me that I ruined supper. I stare at my plate, waiting for a lecture.

"Arlaina, did I not tell you earlier to make sure all of that mess was cleaned up?" Her eyes are squinting at me and her mouth is tight. Dad walks back in.

"Can I ask why the rabbit was in this room in the first place?" He lays his hands on his hips. "I thought we said that was a one-time thing when Patrice dropped her off?"

"I'm sorry, Dad, I thought I cleaned everything up," I mumble.

"I cannot have this rabbit in the same room where I eat my food, Arlaina. It's not the rabbit that's the problem at dinner, it's the poop. And we had a deal. What should I think about this?"

"It was an accident. I said I was sorry."

"You can clear the table. I'll have to think about things."

"You're not giving her away, are you?"

"No, I said I would give you a chance. I'm a little bummed out because your mom made a great dessert, and I was looking forward to it."

"Sorry, Dad."

"If you have any homework, why don't you go get that done? We can have a chat about this some more tomorrow." Dad disappears from the dining room. Mom gets up and gives me a disappointed look before she leaves. I feel bad seeing them both like this. I start to think Patrice probably never let Obeena hop around where they ate food. As I'm taking the dishes to the kitchen, I can hear Mom and Dad in the living room talking about me and Obeena. I feel my eyes getting blurry with tears, but I'm not going to cry. I fill the dishwasher and go upstairs to my room.

When I get to the top of the stairs, I feel the tears come again, but I don't stop them. The hallway gets blurry as my eyes fill up. When I blink, the tears drop down on my skin and wet my cheeks. I go down the hall and stand in front of my bedroom door. But I just stand there and let the tears slide by my nose and slip into the sides of my mouth. I taste the weird saltiness on my tongue. I sniffle for a few minutes, but I don't want Obeena to see me upset. I think back to a video I watched online about animals feeling what their owners feel. I finish crying before I go into my room. I wipe my face with my sweater and open the bedroom door.

Obeena is in her cage hopping around. I stretch out on the floor close to the cage to watch her. Then she sprawls her fluffy body out across the cage. I stick my fingers in between the bars. She hops away and then comes back. I wiggle my fingers around and she sniffs at them. She lets me rub my fingers across her head before she quickly scurries back to the far side of the cage again.

I keep watching while she nibbles on some pellets. For a minute, I wish she could understand human language and I could tell her about being sad. Then I think it's probably better that she can't understand. I would probably say too much about Dad suggesting she go to our grumpy neighbour. Patrice would be really mad if I let that happen.

After the disaster at supper, I'm glad to see the darkness outside my window. I put my pyjamas on, brush my teeth. I sometimes call Tina before I go to bed, so we can talk about what we're going to wear to school the next day or what we plan to do on the weekend. This won't be one of those nights, since I'm not allowed to use the phone. But if I had a cell, I could text her right now and no one would know. Luckily, tomorrow is Saturday, and I'll get to see Tina at some point. I plan to tell her everything. As I climb into bed, I think about how good she is at listening. Even when she can't help me, sometimes it feels better just to talk about stuff with her. Maybe Tina listens to me because she doesn't have any brothers or sisters. With only her and her mom, she doesn't have some of the same problems I do, like with Kyle and my dad. But as much as Kyle is a real pest, I'm glad

I'm not the only kid in the house. Sometimes it's good to have someone else to get into trouble with.

My thoughts make me sleepy and I can feel myself starting to doze as my mind drifts away. I throw my pillow on the floor and pull the blanket to my neck to try and go to sleep. I hear Mom's voice in my head saying tomorrow will be another day. I hope that's true.

CHAPTER 7

The Meeting

I usually don't like Mondays, but when a new student shows up, things turn interesting. It seems kinda late in the year to be starting over at a new school, but here she is, standing at the front of the class beside Mr. Matthews. She's wearing new jeans and a beautiful pink and beige headscarf made of silk. It shines against her tanned cheeks.

Mr. Matthews stretches his arm out toward her. "Let's welcome our new class member, Nadia Shaker, everyone."

"Hi, Nadia," everyone replies almost all at the same time. Nadia gives a quick wave. I'm mesmerized by her smile.

"Her dad is an ambassador. She and her family moved to Canada all the way

from Egypt. Nadia, you can take that empty seat over by the window."

I'm not sure what an ambassador does, but it sounds important. Nadia picks up her book bag and goes over to the desk. She seems interesting and I want to know all about her. She's the first person I've ever met in real life who actually comes from one of the countries in Africa, but I'm too shy to just ask her a ton of questions.

By Nadia's second week here, I've learned that she is not shy at all. She puts her hand up in class all the time. If she thinks something in her mind, she just says it out loud. I like how her accent sounds when she talks. If she walked to school, I could ask her what it's like to live in Egypt. But her mother drops her off and picks her up every day. I know the only chance I'll get to ask her a million questions is if I invite her to hang out at the picnic table with me and Tina at lunchtime.

On Wednesday, I find my chance. Since Nadia's desk is right beside the big pencil sharpener near the window, I come up with the idea to break my pencil lead. While the class is copying notes from the board, I take my pencil over to sharpen it. Nadia's big dark eyes are glued to the board as Mr. Matthews is writing. Today she is wearing a light purple headscarf. It matches the knee patches on her jeans. I think she's so pretty.

"Hi, Nadia." I stick my pencil in the big sharpener and turn the handle.

She looks up at me and smiles. I smile back.

"What is your name again?" she asks.

"Arlaina."

"Oh yes. That's a pretty name. Hi, Arlaina."

"Your name is pretty too."

"Tell me something, Arlaina, where are all the Black kids in this school?"

"There's lots," I tell her. I never thought about how many.

"Where I come from, almost everyone has brown skin. Here, it's so different. Almost everyone has white skin."

I don't know what to say to that but I guess she's right. I'm thinking now is my chance to ask questions.

"How come you came from Egypt? The school year is almost over."

"My father is a diplomat. The government doesn't care if it's the end of school or the beginning of school. If my father gets moved somewhere, we have to go."

"Do you get to travel all over the world?" I want to know more.

"Not all over the world, but I have lived in three different countries in Africa."

"Three countries? Wow!" I take a deep breath in. I'm nervous and I wonder if Nadia even wants to get to know me. I hope she says yes to hanging out. "Do you want to hang out with me and my friend Tina at lunchtime?"

"Okay." I watch Nadia's face light up and I am relieved. I start to grin. Nadia flashes her pretty smile again.

"We usually go to the picnic table by the far end of the fence."

Mr. Matthews notices us talking and calls out.

"Arlaina, how sharp do you need that pencil?" He folds his arms.

"Sounds like someone has a problem with two Black girls talking," Nadia whispers. "Maybe he thinks we're talking about him."

We giggle and I go back to my seat. I like Nadia. Mr. Matthews turns back to the board and erases the work before I'm finished.

"Okay, class, let's look at a math problem. Who wants to come up and solve this one?" Mr. Matthews scribbles the problem on the board. Nadia raises her hand. Mr. Matthews holds out his chalk to her, but Nadia doesn't take it. Instead, she grabs one from the chalkboard ledge and starts writing out the steps. Mr. Matthews steps back and watches her. When Nadia is finished, she puts the chalk back and smiles at her work.

"Thank you, Nadia. But you're not done. What is the missing step right before your last one?"

Nadia picks up the chalk as she thinks about it.

"While you're thinking about that, Nadia, let me ask you, is that headscarf an Egyptian tradition?"

Nadia's mouth falls open. She looks shocked by Mr. Matthews' question.

"Are you serious?" she asks.

"I'm curious. I'm just trying to learn about your culture."

"Well, get a book. You always tell the class to do homework, why don't you go do yours!" Nadia throws the chalk on the ledge and storms back to her seat. Mr. Matthews' face turns red. I love watching how embarrassed he looks. I think the class likes it too. They seem amused by how Nadia put him in his place. I want to be like that. I can't wait until we get to the picnic table at lunchtime. I know she will have something to say about Mr. Matthews.

After the second lunch bell rings, I take off outside with Tina and Nadia. We head straight to the picnic table. Tina and I hop up on top and plant our feet onto the seat part. Nadia doesn't sit down. She also doesn't hold back any of her thoughts about Mr. Matthews.

"Is this the man who is teaching you? He is not too smart." Nadia puts a hand on her hip.

Tina and I giggle.

"Yeah, he's a goof." Tina laughs.

"No, he is much more than that." Nadia isn't laughing. "Arlaina, you should be worried about this teacher. He would never get away with this back in Egypt."

"What do you mean?" I stop laughing.

"Just watch." Nadia calls Chris over. He is one of the Black boys in our class.

"Hey, Nadia." He grins. "You sure told Matthews what's up today."

"Your name is Chris, right?" Nadia responds.

"Yup."

"Tell me, do you think it was wrong for Mr. Matthews to say what he said to me in front of the whole class?"

"I wasn't shocked. He always does stuff like that."

43

"Does he ask the white kids about stuff they wear on their heads? Or about their culture?"

"White people don't even have a culture, do they?" Chris asks.

Nadia and I laugh.

"Hey! I have a culture," Tina whines.

"My bad, Tina. No offence." Chris grins.

"Seriously, we need to do something about Mr. Matthews," Nadia says.

"That's what I've been thinking for a long time, but I don't know what to do or who to tell about it. It'll probably seem like we're just trying to get him in some trouble," I reply.

Nadia puts a hand on the other hip as she thinks.

"Okay, what we need to do is gather some Black kids for a meeting. There has to be other students in the school who have been made to feel bad by this teacher. Maybe in the hallway, or maybe at an assembly or something?"

Chris whips his finger in the air.

"I know I'm one of them. You're probably right, Nadia," he says.

"Okay, let's spread the word and let's meet here tomorrow at lunch to talk about this." Nadia is on a mission. She finally takes her hands off her hips and climbs up on the picnic table between us.

"Yup, sure." Chris waves goodbye and rushes to the basketball court to join his friends. I see him huddling with his three Black friends there. Tina looks worried.

"Are you okay?" I ask her.

"I'm not Black. Am I allowed to go to the meeting too?"

"Are you a snitch?" Nadia asks, giving Tina a grin and a side-eye.

"No."

"Then you can come."

Tina claps excitedly. I don't know what we will talk about or how we will make a difference, but I plan to follow Nadia's lead. She seems to know what she's talking about.

CHAPTER 8

Africa Is Not a Country

It's Thursday, and the rain is drenching me as I walk down Central Parkway to school. Luckily, Mom threw my running shoes in my book bag before I left the house. My black-and-white rain boots are now full of mud from stomping in every puddle on purpose. But I don't care—it's lots of fun. I look up at the dark grey sky and the rain slaps my face. I feel like it's going to start thundering any minute, but I'm still taking my time.

If Mom knew I was fooling around in the rain, she would probably be upset. She doesn't like it when the rain wets my hair. She watched the weather on television last night. When she heard them say we were getting rain, she put Fulani braids in my hair. I didn't mind, because she always braids my hair in cool patterns and designs, and I love it. Plus, I always know why she's doing it. When my hair is open and straightened out, the rain turns it into one giant fuzzy ball.

Mom and Aunt Dottie always say that unwelcomed water is the enemy of a Black girl's hair. Maybe that's why Mom never put me in swimming lessons.

More than once, the rain came without warning, when my hair was unbraided. And every time, I ended up looking like a poodle who just sat under a dryer. Once the rain gets my hair wet, it tangles. It takes a lot of work for Mom to get it back to soft and curly. The puffy poodle look doesn't matter at home and in the shower, but it's a big deal if I'm at school. There are only three other Black kids in my class. Two are boys. Their short afros don't look much different when they're wet, like my longer hair does. And Nadia's hair is always covered with her headscarves. She doesn't have to worry about her hair fuzzing up.

With all the braids and colourful beads in my hair today, I'm not ducking from the rain on my way to school. Mr. Matthews won't be able to make a comment about my hair. The last time it got wet while it was unbraided, Mr. Matthews asked the girl sitting in the seat behind me if she could see the board. I know he was only asking because my hair was all puffed out from the rain. She told him that she could see the board. I think it was rude of him to even ask her that, just like it was rude for him to ask Nadia about her headscarf in front of the class.

The rain starts coming down harder, and some of the kids run past me to get to school and out of the rain. I'm glad there are only a few weeks left before the end of the school year. After that I won't have to get up early and take

47

this walk. Tina and I will make this our best summer ever. Next year we'll be going into grade seven. We won't be the oldest kids anymore. In middle school, we will be the youngest ones. But we both think it'll be exciting to have some older boys to look at in the hallways.

I slap the bottoms of my feet down into each rainy puddle that I pass. I start to speed up a bit. Other kids are still running past me. The bottoms of my pant legs are soaked but I don't care. I try to keep track of how many puddles I step in. Seven, eight, nine. I have to end on an even number—I don't know why. I step into a tiny puddle to make ten.

I usually meet up with Tina when I get to the end of her street, but I don't see her anywhere. She always leaves before her mother goes to work, but when I look down her driveway, her mother's car is already gone. I guess that means Tina didn't wait for me. If her mother gave her a drive because of the rain, she should have told her to pick me up too.

When I get to school, there's almost nobody outside. I know I'm late. I dash up the stairs and swing the front doors open. As soon as I rush in, I crash right into Jonathan, the skinny boy Tina has a crush on. I grab his jacket sleeve to keep from falling, but we both tumble to the floor. My bag goes flying in the air.

"Get off me," he squeals.

I let go of his sleeve. We both get up and shake the wet off.

"You should really watch where you're going, Arlaina."
He scowls at me.

"I'm sorry, it was an accident." I try to fix my book bag
back onto my shoulder.

"You should just go back to your own country," he says.
I don't know what he means.

"Canada *is* my country," I tell him.

"No, it isn't. You just live here. Your people come from
Africa. All Black people come from Africa." He marches
down the hall before I have a chance to say anything else.
I'm so angry, my face is burning. I want to chase him down
the hall and punch him in the face, but I know I will get
in trouble if I start a fight. Now we *really* need to have our
meeting at the picnic table.

I can't figure out how Tina has a crush on Jonathan.
She is the one who puts "blue-eyed" in front of his name
because she likes his eyes. But he's nothing but a jerk. Now
I know why he never speaks to me. And I hope Tina never
speaks to him after I tell her what he said. If I was bold like
Patrice, I would chase Jonathan down the hall and get in
his face. I would shout, even if spit came flying out, to tell
him that he's wrong. Africa is not a country, like Patrice
taught me. Then I would point my finger close to his face
and scream at him that Africa is an entire continent, with
fifty-four countries in it. And if no teachers had broken
me away by then, I would use my angriest voice to make
sure he knows that Canada is *my* country just as much as
it is his.

All the African countries are separate and different. Like where Nadia lived, in Egypt. Her country is not the same as every other country in Africa. Patrice says that all of the countries there have places of great beauty, each with their own cultures and languages and traditions. She says, at one time, they had kings and queens. She knows everything about Africa. And it's nothing like what they show on television. They make it look like all of Africa is one big village with poor people and no clean water. But Patrice says the countries in Africa all have rich people and poor people in them, just like every other place in the world. I already miss Patrice and all the things she teaches me.

When I turn the corner to the classroom, Jonathan is there in the hall. I wish right then that I could say all the things on my mind. But I know the words probably won't come from my mouth the same way they are sitting in my head. I think I would need to punch him first, *then* make him listen.

Jonathan opens the class door and walks in. I slide in right behind him. I can't stop feeling the weirdness inside my body from what he said. I was in a happy mood splashing in those puddles, but now I feel mad, or sad, or embarrassed. Or maybe all of them.

"Stop right there, you two." Mr. Matthews holds his hand up like a crossing guard stopping traffic for kids to cross. Jonathan folds his arms and I notice his dirty fingernails.

THE GROVER SCHOOL PLEDGE

Mr. Matthews comes over to us. He has chalk in his hand, and of course, some chalk in his hair. "Do either of you care to share with the class what major event has you both so late?"

"Mr. Matthews . . ." I start, wanting to explain to him that we didn't come together, but he cuts me off.

"Save the explanation, Arlaina. Everyone else managed to get to class on time. You will both have detention in here with me during lunch hour." He waves his hand for us to go to our seats. I see that Tina is already sitting in hers. She gives me a dirty look when I sit down. She's probably mad because she thinks I walked with Jonathan. Wait until she finds out that her "blue eyes" doesn't like Black people. Mr. Matthews goes back to writing on the chalkboard. Tina scribbles on a piece of paper and passes it to me. I open it up. It says, "Arlaina, you are a boy stealer."

CHAPTER 9

The Crush

"Class, I want to remind you that we have our school assembly coming up. Principal Warren has invited some guests to speak to you older grades to see if any of you would be interested in their summer camp. I think it's a fantastic opportunity to experience some hiking and horseback riding. But most importantly, you get to volunteer helping seniors way out in the country."

"It's out in the woods? No thanks," a student grumbles.

"Regardless of whether you want to go or not, you still have to come to the assembly and listen."

"I think I'll be sick that day," Tina complains. I silently agree. It sounds nice to go and help seniors, but I don't know how I feel about hiking all day and being stuck out in the country with a bunch of horses. I think I would sit in a field with a hundred bunnies like Obeena before I would get on one horse. But maybe if I knew how to ride, I would feel different.

At the bell, everyone rushes to grab their lunch and get back to their seats. I eat my sandwich in silence while everyone else is chatting and laughing and swapping food. I don't feel like talking or trading sandwiches, but I do want to talk to Tina. Every time I look over at her, she turns her back and starts chatting with a girl sitting on the other side of her desk. I thought I would get a chance to tell her what happened with Jonathan, but she is totally ignoring me.

I know that as soon as the second bell rings, everyone will be rushing to get outside for the second half of lunch. But I will be sitting inside with Jonathan. Tina will probably hate that too. I need to try and talk to her before that second bell. I tap her back and she swings around, squinting her eyes at me.

"Why are you acting like a snob?" I ask with an attitude.

"You know why. I saw you read my note."

"Do you think I like blue-eyed Jonathan?" I slap my hand across my forehead, then throw my arms out to the side. Does she really think I'm a boy stealer?

"You came late with him, so that means you guys were walking together." She stops looking at me and slurps from her water bottle.

"I didn't come to school with Jonathan. I walked here all by myself because my friend left me behind this morning." I cross my arms. Tina looks back at me again.

"I didn't leave you, Arlaina. My mom made me hop in the car because it was raining out and she didn't want me to be late."

"Jonathan has nasty, gross fingernails," I blurt out.

Tina gives me another mean look.

"He does not. Take that back," she says.

"He does. How about you watch his hands in gym class later when we do the rope climbing."

Tina is thinking. I can tell she doesn't want to talk anymore. I won't get a chance to tell her what Jonathan said to me. She's so mad, she probably won't believe me anyway. She turns her back again. We eat the rest of our lunch without talking. When the second bell rings, everyone hops up from their desks. It looks like Tina is waving as she leaves the classroom. Maybe she's not mad anymore.

Nadia stops by my desk on her way out.

"I guess we are not going to have our meeting by the picnic table today, then?" She frowns.

"No." I feel bummed out about it and I hang my head.

"I'll let the others know." She throws her lunch wrappers in the garbage and slips out of the classroom.

Soon the room is empty and there's only me and Jonathan left, sitting far across the room from each other. Mr. Matthews sits on the corner of his desk.

"Both of you, come closer. You can sit in these two front seats here." He points.

Neither of us wants to sit next to the other, but we

listen to Mr. Matthews and move to the seats in front of him.

"I hope we don't have to sit like this for the whole detention," Jonathan grumbles.

"This is what happens when you come to school late. Class was already started." Mr. Matthews folds his arms.

"He doesn't want to sit next to me, and I don't want to sit next to him." I frown.

"That's right," Jonathan mumbles.

"What is going on between you two?" Mr. Matthews asks.

"In the hallway, he told me to go back to Africa." I'm angry all over again. Mr. Matthews looks surprised.

"Did you say this, Jonathan?"

Jonathan lowers his head. "Yeah."

"Really? Well, it looks to me like Arlaina isn't too happy about what you said. Do you understand why?" Mr. Matthews asks.

I want to tell Mr. Matthews that he also says things I don't like.

"I was just mad at her," Jonathan answers.

"That's no reason to be awful," I say back. Now is my chance to speak what I feel. "I was born in Canada just like you were. Probably at the same hospital. And so were my parents, just like yours. This isn't just *your* country. I was never in any of the countries in Africa and neither were my parents. Actually, neither were any of my grandparents. We are Canadian. But I can tell you that Africa is a beautiful continent with beautiful people. Maybe I will get to visit some of its countries one day. But you should know what you're talking about before you speak. Telling a Black person to go back to Africa is racist."

"I'm not racist!" Jonathan yells.

"Then stop saying racist things!"

"I see videos all the time. It's all over the internet. So how is that racist?"

I look at Mr. Matthews to help explain. He looks confused, like he doesn't know what to say to Jonathan. I hold my hands out, motioning for Mr. Matthews to say something. He takes a breath in and then lets it out.

"Jonathan, what is it you are seeing on the internet?"

"You know, like all those Black people in those little mud huts. Walking around with those baskets on their heads and hardly no clothes on, and dirty feet."

I had never seen such videos.

"And they always don't have food and stuff," he continues.

Mr. Matthews clears his throat. I'm annoyed that he looks like he is trying to think of a response. I wait to see what he will say.

"First of all, you can't believe everything you see online."

"But they're right there, I can see them. It's not fake."

"That's not the reality of every person in Africa. And I think you owe Arlaina an apology. Africa might be where Black people came from originally, but all of our families come from somewhere else. Mine came to Canada from Ireland about a hundred years ago, and yours came at some point too."

I feel awkward but I have to correct my teacher. "Mr. Matthews, I think First Nations people don't count. They were already here before anyone else ever came. That's what my dad says."

"Yes, Arlaina, your father is correct."

I wonder why Mr. Matthews didn't mention it before I did. He looks kind of embarrassed and runs a chalky hand through his hair.

"So, what about all those things on the internet, then?" Jonathan asks.

"Don't believe it. There are lots of people out there who want to spread lies over the internet." Mr. Matthews raises his hand to his hair again. He clearly wants to be done with this conversation. "Jonathan, do you have something to say?" He folds his arms and glares at Jonathan.

"Sorry, Arlaina," Jonathan mutters. I think he feels bad. I wish Mr. Matthews would feel bad about some of the things *he* says.

"Okay," I respond.

"Good." Mr. Matthews is relieved. "Now, can we finish this detention in silence?"

Jonathan turns red like a tomato and turns his face toward the window. Mr. Matthews starts chuckling. I'm not sure what he finds so funny.

"Oh, I see what is happening here," he says. "I think

someone in this room has a little crush on someone else in this room."

Jonathan puts his head on the desk and hides his face with his arms.

Ew! Jonathan has a crush on me? That's so gross. And now *I'm* embarrassed. I feel like I'm as red as a tomato too, but they just can't see it because my skin is brown. I think about how I would even begin to explain this to Tina.

CHAPTER 10

A Million Men Marching

The house is quiet when I walk in from school. I think maybe I'm home alone for a change, but when I get to the living room, I see Mom, Dad and Kyle gathered around the television. I can tell something serious is happening by the looks on their faces.

"What's going on?" I ask.

"Shh." Dad waves his finger in the air.

"There's a protest downtown," Mom whispers loudly. "And we need to have a talk about your detention later."

"A fifteen-year-old kid got roughed up by the cops," Kyle shouts.

"I said be quiet," Dad says. "The organizer is about to make a speech."

I sit down next to Mom on the sofa and stare at the screen. There is a big mob of people standing in Parade Square chanting and waving signs. Most of them are Black, but I see some white people in the crowd too. I also see some First Nations people. I want to ask Dad a bunch of questions, but I know not to talk while everyone is so focused on the protest.

"We are all here to send a united message to our government and to the world." A woman gestures with one hand as she speaks through the megaphone she's holding in the other. Her hair is wrapped high in an African-patterned headscarf. She is wearing a button that says *We Matter.* Her expression is serious and she reminds me of Patrice. Whenever Patrice talks about injustice, her face gets madder and her voice gets louder.

"We will no longer stand for this cruel and unjustified treatment of our people," the woman continues. The protesters shout in agreement every time she speaks. Dad is glued to her every word.

"How can we sit by in silence while the police terrorize and brutalize our young Black men? Dillan Gray did nothing to deserve the inhumane, violent assault he suffered at the hands of the men and women who are paid to protect us. This could have been your son or mine. Enough is enough!" she yells. The protesters on the television cheer and scream and wave their signs. Dad claps.

I have so many questions to ask him. Why are the police hurting young people? Why do we need to gather in the streets to make it stop? I heard about protests from Patrice, but I don't understand all of it. I know about minorities being treated badly. I've even seen it at school with

Mr. Matthews and a few other teachers who sometimes treat the Black kids differently. But I wonder if all those people and their protests even make a difference. Does that really change anything?

At the dinner table later, Mom and Dad are still talking about the protest. Dad is frustrated about what happened to the Dillan kid. Mom is trying to express to Kyle what he should do if he ever has any contact with the police. I am sitting and listening, just waiting for a chance to get my questions answered.

"I hate that we have to have this kind of conversation with you, Kyle. And even for you, Arlaina. But what happened to Dillan is a reminder that not everything is fair. Our reality is still that not everyone sees us as equal," Mom explains.

"If a cop tries to beat me like they beat Dillan, I will bust them wide open with these iron fists!" Kyle is punching his fists in the air.

"No, son, that's the exact wrong thing to do," Dad says.

"Why? If they can come at me, I'll come right back at them."

"That's what they hope you will do, so they will have a reason to justify their actions," Dad explains. "You gotta be smart, Kyle. You go throwing punches at a cop, they can say you were aggressive, and that they had to handle you. Instead, you do exactly what they ask the whole time, no matter what. As a Black male, you are already seen as a thug, like you're guilty of something. Don't ever allow anyone to attach those labels to you."

"I know it's not fair, so that's why we fight to try and change these things," Mom adds.

"But how does protesting change any of that?" I jump in. Finally, I get to ask a question.

Dad lets out a big sigh. "Let me share a story with you, kids," he says.

"I was probably about your age, Kyle, when I went to Washington, D.C., with my dad back in 1995. That's where he was born, before his family moved to Canada. He took me to a rally called the Million Man March. It was a show of unity and a way to send a message to all Black men to step up and stand up for the Black family. Be the protector.

It was literally over a million men all gathered together. I was so amazed. The reason my dad took me was because he wanted me to never forget the image of all of those Black men standing as one gigantic force. It was like all of those men were there pledging to be better and do better. Very powerful."

"What was it like, that pledge?" Kyle asks. I want to know too.

"Oh, it was incredible. Do you know what it means to pledge? Your pledge is your promise." I think about Dad's words. *Your pledge is your promise.* That's huge.

"And my father was right," Dad continues. "I never forgot that image. I don't think I've ever seen anything in my life like it since then. Imagine, just a sea of Black that stretches as far as you could possibly see and beyond. People from all over and from every coast were there. And I tell you guys this story to show you what real organizing can do. And how powerful we can be if we stand up together. People are still talking about the power of that march, all these many years later. It inspired some of the greatest social-justice activists of all time, including Barack Obama. It even sparked a lot of other big movements."

"You mean like that protest on TV?" I ask.

"Yes, we've changed a lot of things with peaceful protests. Not just in America, but right here too. And that's real talk."

Whenever Dad says "real talk," we know it means something. He is so proud and excited as he's talking, and that makes me excited too. I would love to be a part of something, like Dad was. I believe him when he says that we can change things when we fight for what's right. Even though I'm not quite sure if Tina is still mad at me, I'm so happy and I'm full of ideas. I can't wait until I meet with everyone at the picnic table tomorrow.

CHAPTER 11

On the Ropes

Our first class of the morning is gym. We were supposed to do rope climbing last class, but we had a substitute teacher. She didn't want to set up the ropes, so she went to the equipment room and pulled out two nets and some sticks. She made us play floor hockey while she sat on the stage, texting. The boys were rude and ignored the rest of us, only passing the little orange ball to each other. We complained to the substitute, but she didn't really care. It was the worst gym class ever.

Since we didn't do it last class, I hope today we get to climb the ropes. Everyone in the class loves rope climbing. We compete with each other to see who can get all the way to the top and who has to slide down in shame because they couldn't make it. I know I will make it to the top. Whenever it's my turn, some of the students clap and encourage me. I'm one of the few who always makes it to the top. I just love hearing them cheer me on from below as I get closer. Climbing is one of the things I do best. I think I know how those climbers feel when they reach the top of Mount Everest. It's one of the highest mountains in the world. Rope climbing at school is my Mount Everest.

On the way to gym class, I duck into a hallway bathroom with Tina. I want it to be empty so I can tell her about Jonathan, since there were too many kids around when we walked to school. But there are some girls putting lip gloss on in the mirror when we walk in. They start chatting to us about rollerblading and swim lessons and other things I am not interested in. Tina giggles with them. I think they're boring, so I stop listening.

The girls finally leave. Tina and I go into separate stalls to pee. She finishes before me and dashes out of the bathroom.

"Hey!" I call to her. I wash my hands fast to go catch up. When I get out to the hallway, Tina is standing there, waiting and smiling. Right away I'm annoyed.

"What took you so long?" She grins.

"Sometimes you think your little jokes are funny, but they're really not." I nudge her.

"I know, but I like playing tricks on you. Didn't you think I left without you?"

Since she's laughing, now is a good time to talk about what happened with Jonathan.

"Tina, I have to tell you something about detention."

"Yeah, about my blue-eyed Jonathan."

Ugh, I hate to hear her call him that. Especially after yesterday.

"We didn't walk to school togeth—"

A loud stomping from behind interrupts me. I turn around, and it's Luke Weeks, a kid from class, barrelling down the hall. His thick body is pounding down as he rushes toward us. He bulldozes between me and Tina and grabs Tina's book bag. He keeps running and doesn't look back.

"Oooh, you red-headed weirdo!" Tina screams. "Get back here!"

Tina takes off down the hall, chasing Luke. Her long arms are waving in the air. I can't believe Luke did this. I watch as they both disappear down the hall and turn the corner. I can hear Tina yelling at him. I start walking toward the gym alone. I don't want to get caught up with Luke's pranks. One detention is enough for me.

The class is already in the change rooms when Tina finally comes in. Her hair is messed up and she is trying to pull it into a ponytail.

"What happened?" I laugh.

"I beat Luke up with my book bag when I took it from him."

I slap my hand over my mouth. I've never seen Tina hit anybody. I feel like if I did that, I would be in trouble right away.

Our gym teacher, Ms. Evans, announces that we will be having a game of soccer outside. At first, I groan along with the rest of the class, but I'm not really mad about the change. I love soccer. I just don't want to seem like the only one. Since it's such a sunny day, Ms. Evans says she wants us to enjoy it. When we get outside, Ms. Evans picks two captains to choose who they want on their teams. I end up on Team A with Nadia and Jonathan. Tina is on Team B and she isn't too happy about it. But I don't worry about Tina. I'm too excited to start the game.

We have a lot of good players on Team A. As soon as the game starts, our team scores right away. Tina's team has a hard time scoring on our net even as the game goes on. They are frustrated, especially when our team jumps up and down with the winning score. At the end of the game, both teams fist-bump and we start walking across the field toward the gym doors.

"You played good, Arlaina." Tina whacks my back.

"Thanks."

"So did my blue-eyed Jonathan."

"Tina, you shouldn't like him anymore and you shouldn't call him that."

"Why not?"

This is my chance to tell her what he said. "Did you know he told me to go back to Africa?" I look at her face as we're walking.

"Why did he say that? You never lived in Africa before." Tina tightens her ponytail, which is coming lose. She has no expression on her face, like she doesn't get it.

"'Cause he was being racist."

Tina stops tightening the hairband and stares at me. "Jonathan is racist?"

"I don't know, but maybe."

She takes her hands down from her head. Now she looks really confused. "I thought a racist is someone who hates Black people. Do you think Jonathan hates Black people?"

"Maybe not. I told Mr. Matthews about it in detention and Jonathan apologized."

"If he was a racist, then he wouldn't say sorry."

"Fine. But also, something else."

"What?" she asks as we get farther from the field.

"I think he likes me. But don't be mad, I don't like him back." I grab Tina's hand, so she knows I mean it. She doesn't say anything.

"And besides, you wouldn't want to keep liking a boy with the personality of a toad anyway."

"Who told you that he likes you?" she asks. She slowly pulls her hand away from mine. We keep walking, slightly behind the rest of the class.

"Mr. Matthews. He said something in detention," I finally spill.

"Mr. Matthews? This sucks," Tina whines.

"Don't worry about it. When we get to middle school, there will be lots of boys to crush on. And they'll probably be cooler than 'blue eyes' anyway."

Tina tries to laugh, but I can tell she feels a little sad. I'm glad I got everything out, and I hope she will forget about Jonathan.

At lunchtime, I can hardly eat. Nadia keeps looking over at me and smiling. I think she's even more excited than I am. When the second lunch bell rings, both of us bolt from class and head to the picnic table at the far end of the school ground. Tina is close behind us. I can see Chris and his two Indigenous friends, Robbie and Silas, heading there too. I know Robbie and Silas are still worried about the incident with their teacher a few days ago. She was talking about a new condo being built near our school. Robbie and Silas told the class it was being built on land stolen from Indigenous people. But their teacher shut them down, and they were confused, because they wanted to talk about how the government took their ancestors' land from them. Behind those three guys is Benny, the other Black boy in my class. When we all get to the table, I climb on top. Tina plops down beside me. Nadia stands beside us with her hands on her hips, waiting for the others. When Benny gets close, he has a frown on his face.

"Why is she here?" He points to Tina.

"It's okay, she's cool," Nadia says. "Besides, it's not about us kids, it's about the teachers."

Benny looks like he wants to say something else, but he doesn't. He sits down on the seat and folds his arms. He seems to relax. Soon we are all huddled on top of and around the picnic table.

"So, what's the plan?" Benny asks.

"Yeah. We can't let Matthews keep treating us different," Chris adds.

"It's not just Matthews," Silas says. His hands are shoved in his jeans pockets. "You all know how Miss Bolton didn't want to talk about First Nations people. She's way worse than Matthews. An Asian girl was taking a drink from the fountain and the water splashed on her forehead. Miss Bolton told her she needs to open her eyes."

Chris laughs. "Maybe that's not what she meant."

"Maybe it was," Silas answers.

"So inappropriate." Nadia shakes her head. I know she is really angry because she's using a big word. She is still standing, like she's on guard.

"Huh? I'm confused," Tina says.

I nudge Tina and whisper, "It's rude because many Asians have that eye shape." I don't want her to ask any questions that might make the rest of the group say she doesn't belong. I give her a side look, and she nods back. I think she gets the hint.

"Well, the Asian girl should be here with us too, then," Chris says.

"Yes. Let's ask her to come to our next meeting," Nadia replies.

"What if we do something big during our field trip?" Tina announces out of nowhere. No one really knows how to respond. "You know, the end-of-the-year trip to the zoo?"

"Yeah, we know what you mean, Tina." I try to help out. "I don't think that would really work, though."

"Oh, okay."

"But I *have* been thinking on this, guys." I slap my hands together and fold them under my chin. "I think we need to make the teachers take a pledge!"

Everyone looks at me. When I see their eyes light up wanting more, I keep talking.

"We get every teacher in the school to sign a pledge saying they promise to recognize us and treat us the same way the other students are treated."

"Will we really be able to do anything this close to the end of the school year?" one of the boys asks.

"We are the oldest here," Nadia preaches. "If we make this happen, things will be better for the others after we're gone.

I learned from my father that our struggles—well, grown-up Black people's struggles, I mean—are not for themselves. The fight is for the ones who come after them. So, what we do now will still make a difference after we leave."

Nadia is making a lot of sense to me. She is so smart. We nod our heads as she talks.

"And I like what you've said, Arlaina," she continues. "A teacher's pledge is what we need. We can make a list of questions that they have to answer with yes or no. Something like, 'Have you ever . . . ?'" Nadia's hands are waving around as she talks.

"Okay. So, they answer the questions, then they pledge that they won't do it again? I like it." Chris smiles. Some of the others nod their heads.

"Shouldn't we ask for a meeting with the principal first so we can explain what we want?" Tina asks. I look at Benny and bite my lip.

"You are right, Tina," Nadia says. I'm relieved that Nadia agrees and that Benny doesn't say anything to Tina.

"We can even get Mr. Warren to help us form the questions and the pledge," Nadia says. "He can be the one to get it to every teacher."

"I wonder about including Mr. Warren, though," Chris says. "Do you think we can trust him to do this? Will we get any real help from the office?"

"I hope we will," I answer.

"How will we know that the teachers have taken the pledge?" Benny asks.

We are all silent as we think about it.

"Hey! Maybe we can ask Mr. Warren to get them to sign the pledges at the assembly coming up," I shout. "That way, we can watch them sign it ourselves, all at once."

"Perfect idea." Nadia claps her hands and pulls a piece of paper from her pocket. We clear a spot as she unfolds it onto the picnic table. She pulls a pencil from her headscarf. We all lean over the paper trying to come up with the questions and write out the pledge. We are so excited. When we finally have some things down on paper, we jump up and down and fist-bump each other. Nadia writes all of our names on the bottom of the paper and says she will talk to Mr. Warren about what we want. The lunch bell rings for us to go back inside. We all march back toward the building, feeling strong and brave.

CHAPTER 12

The Green Igloo

"Come and get this bag, Arlaina," Dad calls to me as soon as I walk through the back door after school. I run through the kitchen and peek down the hallway toward the front door. Dad is standing there holding a big white pet store bag.

"Oh, Dad, I'm so happy! You bought this for Obeena?" I rush to grab the bag.

"No," he says. "Your mother left this in the truck and it's in my way. It has a picture of a bunny on the front of it, so I figure it belongs to your fur ball upstairs."

Dad hands me the bag. I look inside and find two packages of rabbit treats and a cube-shaped package. It has a picture of a little white rabbit on it, sitting beside what looks like a circle-shaped igloo.

"By the way," Dad says, "I took a peek at that receipt in the bag. That rabbit is going to cost us a lot of extra money, you know."

Dad is being a complainer. That's what Mom calls him when he tries to talk to her about shopping. I laugh when she calls him cheap. I pull the strange box out of the bag.

"Dad, what is this?" I ask.

"I have no idea."

I rip it from the package. It looks exactly like the picture on the box. It's a see-through, greenish-coloured igloo. What is Obeena supposed to do with this thing?

Mom bought it, so she will know. I find her in the living room, panting and out of breath like a puppy. The coffee table is pushed all the way back against the sofa. Mom is wearing thick red tights and a dark green tank top. Her boobs are bouncing up and down while she's doing jumping jacks. I giggle because her legs look like red hot dogs. The music is pounding and an exercise person is on the TV screen shouting out some moves. Mom notices me laughing and stops. She puts her hands on her hips.

"Can I help you, young lady?" She looks annoyed, but I can't stop laughing. "It's very funny, is it?" Mom isn't smiling.

"Why are you working out, Mom? You're not even fat."

"Working out isn't just about losing weight, Arlaina, it's about being healthy. We all can't be a cinnamon stick like you." Mom plops down on the small piece of the sofa that isn't blocked by the coffee table. She gulps from a water bottle and tries to catch her breath.

"What's this thing?" I hold up the igloo.

"It's supposed to go inside Obeena's cage."

76

I'm totally confused. Mom gulps from the water bottle again.

"For what?" I ask.

"Think of it like me in this room doing exercises and your brother in the kitchen eating all the food out of the fridge. This little gadget is like a bunch of little rooms and tunnels."

"But to do what?"

"Honey, rabbits like to hide in dark places. So I bought that tunnel so she could crawl into it and hide."

"What if she doesn't like it? Or what if she doesn't even know what it's for?" I'm worrying but I'm not sure why. Maybe because I think it looks strange or I can't picture her inside of it.

"Rabbits have natural instincts, which means Obeena will already know what to use that tunnel for. If she doesn't like it, you'll be able to tell."

"How?"

"Well, if she doesn't like it, she just won't go in it. She'll look like she's not interested. She might even drag it around the cage like she's trying to move it out of her way. If any of that happens, then you just take it out."

"Okay. Well, you really know a lot about rabbits, Mom. Did you grow up on a farm?"

"Nice joke, kid. Go put it in her cage and see how she reacts."

Mom hops up and goes back to the exercises. I run upstairs to my room. Obeena is in the cage, nibbling on a carrot stick. I reach in and stick the igloo at the farthest corner of the cage. Obeena hops over to it and starts sniffing. I sit in front of the cage and watch her. She sniffs all around the outside of the igloo. Then she sticks her head in. With one hop, she disappears inside.

I can see her moving around in circles, as if she's checking out how big it is. After a while, she hops back out. I watch her dash over to the other side of the cage, then turn back around and hop into the igloo again. Once more she hops around inside and then rushes back out. She keeps doing this, and it seems like she's having fun. I laugh at how strange it seems that something like this igloo could even be any fun. After a little while, Obeena stretches herself out inside the igloo and stays there. I guess that's my hint to leave her alone.

CHAPTER 13

The Two New Yorks

It's the weekend and I decide to watch animal videos. I start with rabbit videos in case there are some new things I could learn about caring for Obeena. After a while, I switch to cat videos. Some kids in my class have been talking about them. I usually don't get much time to go online, so I'm having a good time laughing at the cats. There is a video of one little kitten who keeps trying to reach for a string dangling off a table. Every time she reaches, she falls over. It's super funny. A white cat with a big flat face and lots of whiskers is next. He is drinking milk, but the milk keeps getting all over his face, even over his eyes. I hold my stomach and laugh out loud. The phone rings just after that video ends. A few seconds later, I hear Kyle squeal.

"Patrice! It's Patrice!"

I run downstairs and bolt into the living room. Kyle is sitting on the sofa in front of the television with his feet up on the coffee table.

"What's it like in New York City?" He beams. "Is it like how they show on TV?" His eyes are wild with excitement.

"Kyle, let me talk to her," I plead.

I grip the end of his shirt and try to pull him toward me to grab the phone. Kyle turns his head away from me so he can keep talking. I reach my arm across his face and hold my hand open. Kyle pushes my hand away and keeps talking.

"You saw the Statue of Liberty? Wow! That must have been awesome!" he yells.

"Kyle, let me talk," I whine.

"Wait your turn, Arlaina!" He scowls at me.

I sit beside him and tap my fingers on my lap. Then I tap my feet on the floor. I'm dying to hear all the stories that Patrice is telling Kyle.

"Uncle Gus said yes? Good, I can come and stay for a few weeks this summer!" Kyle suddenly leaps from the sofa and starts dancing and singing, startling me. "Yes! All right! I'm going to New York City!" Kyle waves a fist in the air. He keeps the cordless phone stuck to his ear as he discos around the living room.

"What about me? Can I go too?" I ask.

Kyle nods his head in my direction and goes back to his conversation with Patrice. I squeal with excitement. We're both going to New York. Kyle sits back down.

"So, is America better than Canada?" he asks.

"How would she know?" I interrupt. "They just got there, dork."

"Patrice, I'll let you talk to Arlaina now, because she's starting to get on my nerves."

Kyle holds the phone toward me. I reach my hand out to snatch it from him. He waits until I almost have the phone, then he tosses it into the armchair across the room. I make a mean face at him as he leaves. He turns around and sees my face, then sticks his tongue out at me. I'm so excited to talk to Patrice that I don't even care about Kyle's tongue. I hop into the chair and grab the phone.

"Patrice!" I squeal.

"Arlaina!" she squeals back.

"I'm so happy to hear your voice."

"I know, me too. I wish you could have come with us for the drive. It was so much fun."

"Oh, Patrice, please tell me all about it."

"Well, when we left Halifax, we drove straight through to New Brunswick. But first we passed through Truro and Springhill and then Amherst. That took us about six hours. Mom and Dad took turns driving."

"What did you see in New Brunswick?"

"Oh, that was pretty boring. From what I could see, New Brunswick is nothing but trees and farms. Maybe that's because we were only on the big highway. But I ended up falling asleep. By the time Mom woke me up, we were at the United States border crossing."

"What did you guys have to do at the border?" I've never been to the border before.

"Dad had to show the border guy his passport and some

papers about his work. Then he showed me and Mom's passports. The guy asked Dad a hundred questions, but Dad knew all the answers."

"What kind of questions?" I want to know everything.

"Like where we were going and why. What address we would live at in New York, stuff like that. Then finally he let us cross over."

"Then you were in New York City?"

"No, silly. Then we were in Maine." Patrice giggles. "After we got through Maine, then we drove through New Hampshire, and then through Boston."

"That sounds like way too much driving." I frown.

"We stopped a lot to eat and take pictures. It was nice. Except we had this U-Haul thing dragging on the back of the SUV, so sometimes it was hard to find places to park."

"So, after Boston, then you were in New York City?" I want her to get to the New York City part. I want to know what it looks like.

"Well, Connecticut first. Then, after we got through there, we entered New York State."

"Wait, New York State? So, there's two New Yorks, then? I'm so confused."

"Arlaina!" Mom calls me from the kitchen, but I don't answer. I want to hear about these two New Yorks.

"Silly cousin! One is the state of New York and the other is the city. You need to learn your geography. Anyway, how is my baby, Obeena?" she asks.

"She's doing great."

"Arlaina!" Mom calls me again.

"I really miss her," Patrice whimpers.

"Don't worry, I'm taking good care of her. Promise." I don't dare tell her about the poop at dinner.

Just then, Mom walks in with a hand on her hip.

"Child, where's your head at? You have a visitor out at the kitchen door." She grimaces.

It must be Tina. She's the only one who comes for me at the back kitchen door.

"Patrice, I've got to go. But will you promise to call me later?"

"I will." Patrice giggles.

I hang up the phone and follow Mom to the kitchen. Tina is standing inside the door.

"Come in. Do you want a snack?" I smile.

"Yup."

Mom disappears from the kitchen. I make peanut butter and jam sandwiches and pour two glasses of orange juice. Tina and I sit at the table and chat about the exciting meeting we had at school.

"Do your parents know about our plan?" Tina asks.

"No, so be quiet about it."

"Okay. I didn't tell my mom either. I think our parents would try to talk us out of it."

"Out of what?" Kyle sticks his nose into the kitchen and into our business.

"We made plans to have the Grover teachers sign a pledge," Tina blurts out.

Kyle crosses his arms. "Ooh, staging a coup, are we?"

"What is a coup?" I ask.

"Duh. An uprising." Kyle shakes his head.

"Yeah, that." Tina grins.

"Bad idea. Really bad idea," Kyle warns.

"No, it's not, Kyle." I'm getting annoyed with him. "You're always being so negative."

"There's a difference between being negative and being smart. And it's not smart to cause a fuss at school."

"You don't even know our plan," I grumble.

"Okay, what's your plan, smarty-pants?"

"We're going to try and get the principal to announce our pledge at the assembly and have the teachers sign it, saying they will treat the minority kids with respect and they will talk about Black history in class."

Kyle laughs. I look at Tina. I wish she hadn't told him anything. When he finally stops laughing, he sits at the table.

"Listen, those teachers don't care about what you have to say. You're just a little Black kid. Plus, you got Tina helping. That's a total joke."

Tina gives Kyle a nasty look.

"Shut up, Kyle! Go find something else to do," I yell. I know Tina wishes now that she hadn't said anything to my brother at all. There was a time when I thought he would be a good person to tell, too, but clearly, I was wrong.

Kyle grabs an apple from the table and smiles. He bites into it and leaves. I start to wonder if Kyle is right. What if this plan doesn't work and we look like troublemakers to

84

everyone? Mom comes back into the kitchen. Tina pretends to start talking about summer vacation, so Mom doesn't catch on that we're planning something big.

CHAPTER 14

Our Happy News

The day of our big end-of-the-year field trip finally comes. I wake up early because I'm just too excited to wait for Mom to wake me. The sun is blazing through my bedroom window. A perfect day for a field trip. All three of the grade six classes are going to the Axeford Zoo. I'm not sure if I'm more excited about the zoo or about not having to sit in class all day. I know Tina is just as excited as me. I think everyone is.

I stretch my arms up and climb out of bed. I look over and see Obeena shoving her empty food dish around the cage. I'm starting to notice that lately her dish is getting empty much faster. I've been giving her bigger amounts of food, but she seems to be eating it as fast as I give it to her.

Dad has complained to Mom that I'm overfeeding her. He thinks we are spending too much money on rabbit pellets and treats. I guess he's right. Obeena seems to eat more and hop less. I reach for the half-empty bag of pellets and fill up her food dish. Obeena rushes to the dish and starts nibbling madly. Mom's been talking about her friend Katrina's baby having a growth spurt, because he's eating more than usual. So, I guess rabbits must have growth spurts too. What Obeena has left in the bag won't last long, so Mom will have to go out and buy some more.

As soon as I shower and get dressed, I rush downstairs toward the front door. Mom yells out to me as I dash past the kitchen. "Hey! Slow down, you speeding little bullet! What about breakfast?"

"I'm not hungry, Mom, and I have to get going! Today is field trip day!"

I bolt out the front door and down the front stairs. Nadia is waiting for me on the sidewalk. It's the first day her mom is actually letting her walk to school with us. We start half walking, half skipping down the sidewalk. As we near Oak Street, we start jogging toward Tina. Nadia holds on to her headscarf as we run.

"Are you as excited as I am?" I ask her.

"More!" Nadia squeaks.

When Tina spots us, she rushes down her driveway. We all hug each other and scream.

Four yellow buses are pulling up in front of the school as we arrive. The bus in the front parks right at the entrance. The driver shuts off the engine, takes out a newspaper and starts reading. He notices us giggling and jumping up and down. He waves at us as we pass to go inside the building. We decide we will rush to the front of the lineup so we can get a three-seater on the friendly man's bus.

Inside the school is chaos. The sixth-graders are noisy and hyper. Principal Warren calls our three classes down to the gym over the loudspeaker. When we get there, he is standing with a mic in his hand. We sit down on the cold gym floor. Mr. Warren tries to quiet the students down, but we are way too excited. Finally, he yells into the microphone and we all stop talking. The gym is silent.

With all the excitement about the field trip, I completely forgot that Nadia had plans to talk to the principal until she whispered to me and Tina.

"Mr. Warren read our note a few days ago and he thinks it's a great idea." Nadia smiles. "He was surprised when I told him how some of us are feeling. He wants to meet with us before the assembly so we can share our experiences with him. We will get to say some words at the assembly. He's going to read our questions out loud, then have the teachers come to the front and sign our pledge in front of the students. Isn't that perfect?"

We both hug Nadia.

"Wow, I can't believe this," I whisper back to her. It's hard to describe the feeling, I just know it feels really good.

"This news *and* field trip day? I'm so happy!" Tina adds.

"Okay, listen up, sixth-graders!" Mr. Warren's voice interrupts our joy. "I know you are all thrilled, but please remember that you are representing Grover out on your field trip today. I expect every one of you to be on your best behaviour. Your teachers have put a lot of effort into making this a great day. And now that we are very close to the end of the school year, as well as your final days with us, we want you all to leave here with some really terrific memories . . ."

"Yeah, yeah, butt breath!" Duncan Turner yells. Duncan is from one of the other sixth-grade classes. Everyone calls him a bully. He laughs out loud at his own rude comment. He is sitting cross-legged behind me and Tina and Nadia. I turn around and glare at him, to make sure he can see that I am irritated.

"What are you staring at, poop breath?" He scowls at me and shows me his fist.

I want to whack him, but if I do, I won't get to go on the field trip. I decide not to waste my time on him. I turn back around to face the front. I'm not afraid of Duncan, but I know I will need to stay far away from him at the zoo. Knowing how much he bullies, he may try to come at me just for making a face at him.

When Mr. Warren finally dismisses us from the gym, we hop up and sprint to be first in line. There is a lot of pushing and shoving to get out of the double doors. The teachers and parent chaperones are trying to keep everyone calm, but there's no order. Everyone wants to get outside to the buses. It's no better when we get outside. There's still a lot of shoving, but somehow we are able to get a three-seater at the back of the friendly man's bus.

Once everyone is seated, Mr. Matthews gives us a lecture about good behaviour. He tries to repeat what Mr. Warren already said, but no one is listening. Finally, the four buses pull away.

CHAPTER 15

Road Claim

"I choose blue," Tina squeals. She wants to play the game we always play whenever we drive anywhere together.

"What do you mean? Blue for what?" Nadia asks.

"It's a game," Tina explains. "It's called Road Claim. We pick a colour and then yell out 'claim' when a car that colour passes by. Whoever claims the most cars by the time we get to where we're going is the winner."

Nadia looks confused. "That's not fun," she says.

"Yes, it is, and it makes the drive go by faster," Tina bites back.

The bus is barely off the school grounds when Tina starts darting her eyes around, looking through the bus windows for blue cars. Nadia shakes her head. She thinks the game is silly.

"I claim that blue truck!" Tina calls out as we pass a blue pickup pulling into the school as we are leaving.

Nadia snickers.

"You're playing, right, Arlaina?" Tina looks at me.

I'm not sure if I want to play. I don't want Nadia to think I'm silly, like the game. It was something we invented when we were younger. Me and Tina used to play it whenever we were in the back of one of our parents' cars. But I almost wish Tina hadn't brought it up in front of Nadia. She thinks it's foolish. I don't want to disappoint Tina, so I decide to play it with her. But I give Nadia a look to let her know that I really don't want to.

Tina pulls a piece of scrap paper and a pencil from her bag. She writes both of our names on the paper and draws a line down the middle. Then she puts a mark under her name for the one point she got from the blue pickup truck. I twist the side of my mouth. Tina is all the way into the game for the whole drive. She gets impatient when I'm talking to Nadia and not paying attention to counting cars.

"Why don't you tell her how childish this game is?" Nadia whispers. We both laugh, but I turn my head and cover my mouth with my hand, so Tina doesn't think I'm laughing at her. I know how much she loves playing the game with me.

When the buses pull into the zoo parking lot, Tina counts up the points.

"I got twenty-five and you got ten," Tina brags but looks disappointed.

I don't usually get such a low number, even when we are just going to the mall. She knows I was barely trying.

"I let you win," I say.

Tina grins then jumps up and down in our seat. She claps for her victory. Nadia is amused.

As the bus comes to a stop, Mr. Matthews stands up.

"Okay, everyone, when the bus door opens, please exit in a rational fashion. We are here to *see* the animals not *be* the animals," he shouts.

"Wow." Nadia shakes her head. "Did you just call us animals? And what is a rational fashion?" she asks.

Mr. Matthews glares at Nadia.

"Step off the bus like your parents taught you how to behave. That's rational fashion," he barks.

When the bus door opens, everyone shoves their way to the front. The two parent chaperones try to help Mr. Matthews, but again, no one is listening to what they're saying. Everyone starts charging off the bus and rushing over to the zoo employee standing there waiting to greet us. As I walk up the aisle, Duncan sticks his foot out and trips me. I fall forward and right into Jonathan, of all people.

"Hey!" Jonathan howls.

"Sorry, I was tripped." I grab onto him to steady myself.

Duncan roars with laughter. I give him a death stare as I fix my clothes, but he doesn't seem to care. He keeps laughing. I leave space between me and Jonathan as we're getting off the bus.

"Hello, everyone, and welcome to the Axeford Zoo. I'm Bennett," the zoo employee announces, "and I'm going to give you all a quick rundown of some of our rules before you go in."

I spot Duncan staring at me out of the corner of my eye. I have a bad feeling in my stomach. I know he's going to keep tormenting me on the trip because I gave him that mean look in the gym. When we get inside the zoo area, Duncan is in a different group than I am. I feel relieved that I won't have to be stuck with him, and I start to relax.

Everyone seems to be having a fun time going from section to section, staring at all the different kinds of animals there. A black jaguar walks over to meet us at the high fence as we get close to it. He walks back and forth in front of us like he owns the entire zoo. Only the wires stand between us and the jaguar.

"He looks so fierce." I grin.

"Yeah, and he looks like he wants to eat us," Nadia says.

We laugh. Some of the students stand farther back. They don't want to come too close to the jaguar, even though he's behind the fence. I'm fascinated by his teeth and jaws. I imagine them chomping down on his prey and shredding its body into tiny little bits. I can imagine the jaguar standing over the dead body with blood dripping from the sides of its mouth. He's staring into my eyes and I'm mesmerized by him. Tina pulls me away from the fence.

"Let's keep moving," she says. "This guy looks kind of mean."

I follow her and Nadia as we try to catch up with the rest of our group. I can't wait to see what else we will meet up with in this zoo.

CHAPTER 16

The Chamber of Doom

So far, our field trip is going well. I'm totally into these animals. Especially the baby ones, stuck to their mothers and following them around. Maybe I like them best because I have one at home that I'm taking care of too. I keep falling behind my group because I stand and stare at the baby animals too long. I watch them with their mothers to see how they act with each other.

I think the tigers would probably be in those safaris that Patrice talks about. She says one day she will travel to Africa and visit countries like Kenya and Madagascar and Tanzania to see the animals in nature. She doesn't like how humans keep them caged in a zoo. But this could be the closest I ever come to seeing them up close, so I plan to take my time and watch all of them.

When we get to the lions, they look lazy. They are all lying around doing nothing. I watch for a minute to see if one of them will get up and come toward me, but none of them do. I stand there for a bit longer. When I turn, I notice my group has disappeared down the path. I run to catch up again. When I get to them, I notice that our group has almost blended in with Duncan's. I start to panic, but then I see that Duncan is walking right next to his teacher. My bones relax. I mix in with my group so that he doesn't notice me.

When we come to a section that houses the monkeys, the boys get really excited for some reason. I suspect it's because monkeys are known to goof around. So are most of the boys in my group. I notice that Jonathan keeps looking at me. I pretend not to notice him. I don't want him to like me. Tina is my friend and that would really make her feel sad.

"Look what those two monkeys are doing!" One of the students points and laughs.

Everyone turns. A few monkeys are picking things from each other's hair and eating them. Others start to laugh too.

"Now, class." Mr. Matthews speaks with his arms folded. "This is simply an act of nature. Those monkeys are grooming each other. Keeping each other clean. It's also how they bond."

Once he explains what they are doing, we stop laughing. As we stand and stare at them grooming each other, a loud squeal comes out of nowhere. We all turn to look, and there is Duncan standing almost directly behind me, wailing out loud. I didn't even realize he was there. He's holding his belly like he's in pain. The adults rush to him. No one is paying attention to the monkeys anymore.

"Duncan, are you okay?" his teacher asks.

Duncan is acting like he can't get his words out. We stand there waiting to hear what he has to say.

"I . . . she . . ." He tries to point.

"Take your time, Duncan. Do you need to sit down?" Mr. Matthews asks.

"She . . ." Duncan looks right at me. I squish up my face because I'm confused.

"That girl just kicked me really hard between my legs!" he cries.

Everyone looks over at me. I'm sure they can see the shock on my face. I can't believe Duncan is really this evil.

"Arlaina?" Mr. Matthews glares at me. There's anger in his voice. He automatically believes Duncan over me. At first, I don't respond. Duncan is known to be a troublemaker at school. I just can't figure out how he could lie so easily. Tina and Nadia stare at me. They are probably wondering if I really did something to him. But if I was planning to, I would have told them. Duncan's teacher is holding onto him and rubbing his back. His howling sounds real, but I know it's fake.

"He's lying!" I blurt out.

"Everybody knows Duncan's a liar," Tina adds.

"Look at him. He doesn't even have any tears," Nadia points out.

The teachers don't look convinced.

"Aww! It really hurts!" Duncan cries out some more.

"Okay, that's it. Arlaina, do you want to explain why you did this?" Mr. Matthews pushes his glasses back and puts his hands on his hips again. Duncan's teacher guides him to a nearby bench and sits him down.

"I didn't touch him, Mr. Matthews. I swear."

"Then what happened?"

"I didn't do anything." My voice sounds weak. Why won't anything else come out of my mouth? If there weren't so many people staring at me, I could concentrate on what I need to say.

"This kind of behaviour is unacceptable for a Grover student." Mr. Matthews shakes his head. He needs to think about what's acceptable for a Grover teacher. It can't be to only believe the white kid. I want to say that, but I don't.

"You didn't see me do any-thing, Mr. Matthews, so how can you just take his side?"

"Because I'm standing right here looking at him. He's in pain."

"Yeah, fake pain," Nadia calls out.

"This is ridiculous," I complain. It's hopeless to argue.

"I'm sorry, Arlaina, but you're going to have to sit the rest of the trip out on the bus. I'm very disappointed in you."

Some of the students gasp loudly, including Tina and Nadia. They are as surprised as I am. Duncan is still holding his belly and pretending to cry. I notice that he never holds his hands anywhere between his legs, where he actually said I kicked him. I wonder if the teachers see that, too, or if they are pretending not to. Mrs. Kelsey, from one of the other sixth-grade classes, offers to walk me back and chaperone me as I sit out my punishment on the bus. I cross my arms defiantly.

"This is not fair," I mumble. I follow Mrs. Kelsey back to the big yellow chamber of doom.

I look back and wave at Tina and Nadia. They wave back. Both look sad. I give Duncan one last death stare as I pass by the bench he's sitting on. He smirks. I am boiling with anger.

"Do not make eye contact with Duncan," Mrs. Kelsey warns. "I think you've caused enough trouble for today."

When we get on the bus, Mrs. Kelsey sits in the front seat and starts up a conversation with the friendly bus driver. I walk back to the seat that I shared with Tina and Nadia. I slide over to the window and put my knees against the back of the seat in front of me. If I stay awake staring out the window at the cars in the parking lot, I'll only think about what I'm missing inside the zoo. So instead, I curl myself into a ball, put my book bag under my head for a pillow and close my eyes. I'm hoping that when I wake up, I will be home in my room with my rabbit.

CHAPTER 17

The Fiasco

I don't know how long I was sleeping on the bus, but I wake up to Mrs. Kelsey and the bus driver laughing loudly, and Jonathan standing by my seat. Why is he even on this bus right now? He should be with the class.

"Hi." I wipe spit from the side of my mouth and sit up. Jonathan slides into my seat. Mrs. Kelsey and the bus driver are still chatting.

"Sorry you got in trouble," he says.

"It's okay. I know I didn't do anything wrong."

"Yeah, Duncan is a real prize."

"How come you're on the bus?" I ask. I shift awkwardly in my seat.

"Mr. Matthews sent me. I'm being punished too."

"For what?"

"I punched him."

"What? You punched Duncan?" I grin.

"Yeah. I knew you didn't kick him."

"Thanks. But why did you do that?" I'm glad someone got Duncan, but now Jonathan is in trouble too.

"I heard him brag about getting you sent to the bus, so I had to get him back for you. Plus, I guess I was kind of mean to you before. So maybe that's why I did it too."

"Thanks," I say again. I try not to look at his hands, but I can't help it. He looks kind of embarrassed. He picks at his fingernails. Then he sits on his hands.

"Now I'm in serious doggie doo." He laughs and I chuckle with him.

Shortly after, the screeching sounds of rowdy sixth-graders pound in my ears as they load onto the bus. Jonathan hops up and goes to his original seat. Everyone is giving him high-fives and fist-bumps as they pass down the aisle.

"Hey, Arlaina, you missed the best part of the trip!" someone shouts.

"Yeah," says another. "Duncan got sucker-punched by Jonathan! You missed it!"

"No sweat. I didn't care," I lie. I am bummed out that I didn't get to see it happen. But from all the excitement, it sounds like everyone is happy that Duncan got whooped. I smile.

For much of the drive back, Tina rambles on about how cool it was that Jonathan stood up to Duncan. I wish she would stop talking about Jonathan.

"I don't care what you say about him, Arlaina. This just

makes me like Jonathan even more," Tina gushes. Nadia sees
me roll my eyes. She shrugs her shoulders and laughs.

At dinner, Mom and Dad keep drilling me about the field
trip. I keep avoiding their questions so I don't have to tell
them I spent most of the trip sleeping on the bus. I know I
will have to say something. The school will let them know
anyway.

"These non-answers don't sound like the exciting field
trip that you rushed out the door for this morning," Mom
says.

"Yeah, you've been going on about this trip all week."
Dad wrinkles his forehead.

"Didn't you enjoy yourself, honey?" Mom asks.

"I was, until this boy lied and said I kicked him. Then I
got sent to the bus."

"Oh, that must be why there's a voicemail on the phone
from your school," Mom says.

"Probably."

"If the boy lied on you, why were you the only one
punished?" Dad asks.

"Mr. Matthews didn't believe me."

Dad sighs.

I'm glad when nighttime finally comes. As soon as I lie
on the pillow, I feel like I want to cry. I think it's because I
wanted to cry on the bus and didn't. The trip I waited for

all year turned out to be a fiasco. A disaster. And the worst part is I didn't even get to see the place where the rabbits are kept.

I think about Jonathan punching Duncan. I'm sure Tina doesn't know that he did it for me, and I won't be the one telling her. She would probably think I'm bragging. But that's just gross. It's weird that Jonathan likes me. It's even more weird that Tina still likes him anyway. I close my eyes so I can sleep and stop thinking about Tina and Jonathan. I guess that's a different kind of fiasco.

CHAPTER 18

My Big Old Bunny

As I'm lying in bed, I can hear the morning rain pounding against my window. It's annoying. I already knew it was going to be a wet weekend, so I don't even rush to get out of bed. I just lie there and listen to the sounds. If the sun would shine through the curtains, I would get out of bed in a happier mood, especially after the field trip went so wrong yesterday. But I can't stop the rain. I wish I could. Tina and her mom have plans to drive to Orangeville to visit Tina's grandfather. Nadia is supposed to attend a gathering with her parents and some people from her father's work. So my plan will be to play with Obeena all day.

Finally, I crawl out of bed and head downstairs in my pyjamas. Mom is cleaning the kitchen.

"Hey, sleepyhead, do you want to make cookies today?"

Normally, I love baking with Mom. I especially love

eating pieces of the cookie dough. But today I'm not in the mood for either.

"Not really. Can we bake them tomorrow?"

"Okay. Are you all right?"

"Just thinking about yesterday."

"Oh, honey. You know what I always say, tomorrow is a new day. Ooh, that rhymed!" she chuckles. Her giggly mood is cheering me up.

"So even though it's raining, let this be a new day. Milk and homemade cookies?"

Mom pats my scattered curls down with her hand.

"Okay." I smile.

As soon as our cookies come out of the oven, Dad and Kyle rush into the kitchen.

"We smelled these from outside." Dad grins.

They both grab a handful of cookies and start munching. Mom and I pour some milk and sit at the table.

"Been thinking about what you told us, Arlaina." Dad is standing at the counter, stuffing a cookie in his mouth. "You know, about your problem with that bully." He swallows the rest of the cookie before he finishes talking. "I believe you when you say you did nothing wrong. And when things happen that are not fair, you have to stand up for yourself. You have to use your voice."

I take a big gulp of my milk and nod my head in agreement. Dad is right. I need to use my voice.

* * *

When Sunday comes, I wake up early for church. I step out of bed and pull the curtains back. It's still raining. As I'm searching through my closet for something to put on, I can hear Mom and Dad buzzing around, getting ready. I grab a blue blouse and a long, black skirt and start getting dressed. Kyle is loudly belting out some church hymns. I think it's about time we tell him that his singing is really horrible.

At church, all the seats are filled, as usual. Mom comments that the choir is "full of fire" as she claps her hands to the beat of their song. The music has people jumping from their seats, singing and dancing around. I watch the drummer. His sweat is flying as he pounds out the beats. The bass player is hopping around on the stage. His long braids are swinging all over the place as he strums his heart out. One of the elders who always dances steps into the aisle and starts to give us a show. She dances up and down the aisle, screaming and singing along with the choir. People grin and clap in her direction. A few jump into the aisle and dance with her.

This mayhem happens every Sunday and I love it. It's exciting. Mom says a lot of Black churches are like this. Once the choir finishes their selection of songs, the pastor tries to settle everyone down. That's always a struggle, but then everyone is quiet. He tells us to turn to a chapter and verse in the Bible. Just as the pastor is about to read the passage aloud, Dad's friend Jeff Blockhouse stands up. He looks around the church and says that he wants to confess his sin. Kyle starts grinning in his seat. He's anxious to hear the news. Mom gasps and presses her hands over my ears. I fold my arms and try to squirm away from her grip. I want to hear about Jeff's sin too.

Through my plugged ears, I can hear the muffled sounds of Jeff talking about Katie Will. She's one of the second-grade teachers at my school. When he's finished talking, Mom takes her hands away from my ears. She looks angry and whispers to Dad. "Using church service to air his dirty laundry? He really needs to go take that mess to the Lord in prayer."

Dad shrugs his shoulders. He looks a little embarrassed. I try to get Kyle to tell me what Jeff said, but he won't. My guess is that Jeff kissed the teacher and his wife got mad. Why else would he need to confess?

On our way home from church, we stop to pick up Tina. I'd invited her for Sunday dinner at my house since we didn't get to hang out on Saturday. When we get home, Tina and I go straight up to my room. Tina lets Obeena out of her cage while I change out of my Sunday clothes. Obeena hops around the room. Tina sits on the floor and watches her.

"She's getting so fat," Tina comments.

I throw my church clothes on the bed and pull on a pair of jeans and a T-shirt.

"I know. She's been eating everything in sight." I join Tina on the floor.

"How come?" Tina asks.

"I don't know. She's just always hungry."

Obeena hops around us as we talk.

"I think it's cute that she's getting so chunky. But maybe you're overfeeding her."

"Overfeeding her? I am not! I can't just let her starve."

"But you don't have to give her food every second either. Suppose she gets so fat she can't even hop around anymore?"

I laugh. "That will never happen, Tina."

"Remember what we learned in health class? A good diet and exercise keep your body strong and your heart healthy."

I roll my eyes at Tina, who's trying to sound like a commercial. "That's for humans, not rabbits."

"Jonathan got suspended for one day for punching Duncan," Tina blurts. I already know.

"Yeah." I cross my legs to make room for Obeena to hop past me.

"Poor Jonathan." Tina shakes her head.

"Yeah, poor Jonathan." I don't want to say much more. "But he made his choice. We can't worry about him. We have to worry about the pledge."

"Well, you said no to my idea and now we're doing yours. There's nothing to worry about, right?"

I guess Tina feels some kind of way about my comment at the picnic table. But her idea to do something at the zoo was a bad one. And it turns out, I would have missed the whole thing anyway. Maybe she's hoping my idea doesn't work either.

Tina reaches over to pick up Obeena, but she hops away and dashes into the cage.

"Look. I'll bet she wants more to eat," Tina jokes.

"Stop making fun of her, Tina."

Obeena goes straight to the food dish and nibbles on pellets. Tina laughs again.

"See, Arlaina? I told you. Soon she's going to be the size of *two* rabbits."

Tina is still giggling about it when we go downstairs for dinner. She even giggles randomly when we're at the table eating.

"All right, Tina, let us in on the joke," Mom finally says. "What's so funny?"

"It's Obeena. I can't get over how chubby she is."

"And how much money she's costing," Dad adds.

"I hadn't really noticed her getting bigger," Mom says. "But as long as she's healthy . . ."

"Do you think Arlaina is feeding her too much, Mrs. Jefferson?"

"No I'm not!" I shout.

"You are!" Tina shouts back.

"Am not!"

"Uh-oh! Cat fight!" Kyle grins.

"Girls! Girls!" Dad holds up his hands. "I don't want to listen to the two of you arguing about the size of a rabbit!

This is Sunday dinner, it's supposed to be peaceful. Can we enjoy it?"

"Besides, she's a growing bunny," Mom adds. "She's having a growth spurt maybe. She's got to grow somehow."

No one says anything.

"Maybe you should take her to the vet," Kyle pipes up. "She might be suffering from boragorbia!"

"Boragorbia? What's that?" Tina asks. I wish she hadn't asked.

"That's when you gain weight by being so boring!" Kyle bursts out laughing.

Dad is amused by Kyle's unfunny joke. Mom glares at Dad and he stops smiling. I feel like I have to say something.

"Everybody ignore Kyle."

"Maybe we should just take her to the vet for a check," Mom says.

"More money?" Dad frowns.

"Just to make sure everything is okay."

"How much is this going to cost?" he asks. Mom ignores the question. So do I.

"I'll make an appointment for Dr. Fanning to see her. She's my old school friend, and she owes me a favour anyway." Mom smiles.

"Oh, can I come along?" Tina raises her hand like we are in class.

"Sure, as long as your mother says it's okay," Mom answers. "I'll see if we can get her in for tomorrow after school."

The side of Dad's mouth curls up. Favour or not, I can tell he's still thinking about the money. But I'm thinking about Obeena. I hope there's nothing wrong with her. I want to hear the vet tell us it's just a normal growth spurt like Mom talked about.

CHAPTER 19

Good Vet, Bad Vet

At school, all Tina can talk about is us going to the vet after class. But I'm thinking about the teacher's pledge. I'm glad Mr. Warren plans to include us in the assembly. I think about what I will say. I let those thoughts fill my head so I won't think about the visit to the vet, but Tina doesn't let me forget.

"I've never been to a real vet before," she screeches as we move outside for recess. Nadia has pains in her stomach, so she doesn't come outside with us.

"I only went one time," I tell her.

I was with Patrice and her parents, camping in the middle of nowhere, when their dog, Diamond, took off into the woods. Uncle Gus eventually found him moaning and full of quills. He had encountered a porcupine. Poor Diamond was in such pain. I went with Patrice and her parents when they took her to the vet. We watched as he removed the sharp quills from Diamond's fur and paws. This vet was kind and careful. I don't know what to expect with Mom's friend. I hope she's good and I hope she knows a lot about rabbits.

Tina climbs up on the big rock close to our picnic table. I climb up behind her.

"I wonder what the vet office looks like inside," Tina says. "I wonder if there will be rows and rows of cages lined up. All filled with pets waiting for a home."

"I think that's called an animal shelter." I grin.

"So, it's not like in the movies?" she asks. I grin again but Tina is actually serious.

"Arlaina, didn't you ever see that movie *Vets for Pets*? It's where those two veterinarians open up a hospital for sick animals."

I shake my head. I give her a look, so she knows I don't want to hear the story, but Tina tells it anyway.

"So, the two guys in the movie aren't real vets. They're pretending so they can scam pet owners for their money. People drop their sick pets off, but when they come back, the pets are hidden in the back."

I jump down from the rock. I'm done with hearing about some weird movie. Tina hops down behind me and keeps talking. "So then the vets clean the animals up right before their owner shows up. They pay a bunch of money for the vet bill, but their pet isn't better. The fake vets just take their money."

"C'mon, Tina. Couldn't they tell their pet was still sick? The movie sounds cheesy."

"Well, the pets look better because they're clean. But after they get home, their pets get worse. When they go back to complain, the vets lie and won't give the money back."

"Boring!" I say. But it makes me think about taking Obeena to the vet. I hope the visit turns out okay.

"Well, the guys get caught in the end and they have to pay all that money back."

"Please say that's the end." I smirk.

"Wow, you don't have to be so rude."

I smile so Tina doesn't feel bad, but I'm glad it's the end.

After school, Tina and I go straight to my house. She's really excited and that makes me feel less nervous. Mom is taking dishes out of the dishwasher when we walk in. I see a small, grey animal carrier sitting on the floor by the pantry.

"Is that for Obeena?" I ask.

"Yes. Why don't you and Tina take it upstairs and put her inside it, while I put the rest of these dishes away? When I'm finished, we can leave."

Tina and I rush upstairs with the carrier. Tina holds it open while I take Obeena out of her cage. As I'm scooping her up, I look over at the green igloo. When I see what's inside of it, I scream and almost drop her.

"What's wrong?" Tina asks.

I can't seem to get the words out. I put Obeena back in the cage and cover my mouth with my hand.

"What?" Tina asks again.

"Mom!" I scream. "Mom, come quick!"

Mom rushes up the stairs. Tina is still trying to figure out what's wrong. I point at the green igloo.

"My gosh, Arlaina, what is it?" Mom is alarmed.

"Look—in there!"

Mom and Tina bend down at the same time and look inside. Tina shrieks when she sees huge patches of Obeena's fur balled up in the corner. It looks like she was in a fight with another animal or something.

"Obeena's dying," I announce.

"Oh, poor Obeena," Tina moans.

Mom rises to her feet.

"Arlaina, I'm sure Obeena's not dying," she says. "We're going right to the vet, so we'll just tell Dr. Fanning about the fur when we get there, okay?"

Mom picks Obeena up and puts her in the carrier. Obeena squirms.

"See, does she look sick to you?" Mom asks. "This rabbit is very squirmy. She seems totally fine."

The drive to the vet is mostly silent. I don't have much to say because I'm too worried. Tina can tell that I don't want to talk, so she isn't chattering like she always does. I think about the pledge and Kyle saying it's a bad idea. I sure hope he's wrong about that. When I finally get the pledge out of my mind, I start to wonder what kind of disease Obeena might have. I picture Mom and Dad having to pay a lot of money for her to get better. I picture Patrice wishing she hadn't left her rabbit with me. When we pull into the vet parking lot, Mom grabs the carrier. She knows I'm worried because I didn't talk in the car. She brushes my curls with her hand and smiles.

"Don't worry about a thing, it's going to be fine." Mom makes me feel calmer as we head into the vet's office.

CHAPTER 20

Surprise, Surprise

I'm not sure what to think when we walk into the vet's office. There are some people sitting in the waiting area with their pets. The office is loud and disorganized. There are posters on the walls of animals who need families. Along one side of the office is a shelf with pet food and pet supplies for sale. I see pamphlets sitting in pouches labelled *Pet Care*. The receptionist at the front desk smiles at us. Her long, brown hair is pinned back with an orange headband.

"Hello," she greets us.

"Hi." Mom smiles back at her. "We have an appointment with Dr. Fanning."

"Is this Obeena?"

"Yes."

"Okay. Fill out this form while you wait. There's some information we need to know about her. If you aren't sure about some of the answers, just fill in what you know."

Mom takes the clipboard from the secretary, and the three of us sit with the others in the waiting area.

"Just bring it back over when you're finished," the receptionist says.

Mom starts filling out the form. An older woman with white hair is sitting across from us with a beige puppy in her lap. She leans over and is surprised to see Obeena in the carrier.

"Oh, you've got a bunny in there. Look, Sula!" she says to her puppy. "Obeena is a rabbit."

Her puppy leaps out of her arms and starts barking at Obeena's carrier. I move it closer between me and Tina. The puppy keeps barking. Mom picks up the carrier and sets it down on the empty chair beside her.

"Get over here, Sula!" the woman calls. Her puppy stops barking and sits at her feet. The receptionist calls Sula's name. The woman grabs her puppy and follows the receptionist into the back. When Obeena's name is finally called, we follow the receptionist into the back room. It's tiny. There is a desk where the vet keeps her calendar and pens. In the corner is a high table.

I notice a poster on the wall. It's an illustration of a cat skeleton with all its inside body parts labelled. I tap Tina's arm and point to the poster. We both make a face at the disgusting picture, then we laugh. When Dr. Fanning walks in, Mom leaps from her chair.

"Anita!" Dr. Fanning squeals.

"Caroline Fanning!"

They swing their arms open and hug each other. At first, they don't pay any attention to Obeena. They're too busy talking about how good the other one looks and how long it's been since they've seen each other. I wish they would get on with the visit.

Finally, Dr. Fanning takes Obeena out of the carrier. While she's examining her, she asks Mom tons of questions. Then I tell Dr. Fanning about all the fur I found in Obeena's igloo.

"That sounds about right," Dr. Fanning says. I look over at Tina. We are both confused. Dr. Fanning smiles and places Obeena carefully back into the carrier.

"Well," she starts, "you were right to bring her in today, that's for sure."

Oh no. Here comes the bad news.

"You do have a serious issue on your hands here, folks," Dr. Fanning says.

"Really?" Mom sounds worried. I'm worried too.

"Definitely. There's a reason why Obeena has gained this weight and why you found those mounds of fur in her cage."

"Why?" Tina asks.

"Obeena is pregnant. She's going to have some little bunnies soon." Dr. Fanning smiles.

"Pregnant?!" The three of us shout it out at the same time. I said it the loudest.

"My goodness." Mom slaps her hand to her forehead.

"But why is all her fur falling out?" I ask, still stunned.

"Oh no, young lady, her fur isn't falling out. She's pulling it out."

"Eeeww." I look at Tina. She sticks her tongue out like she's about to puke.

"Why is she doing that?" Tina asks Dr. Fanning.

"Because when a rabbit is about to give birth, she begins to prepare a warm place for her babies. Sometimes they use some of their own fur to make the bed cozy and soft. It doesn't hurt her."

I'm amazed by all this. I wonder how Obeena even knew to do something like that?

None of us are saying anything, so Dr. Fanning continues. "What you all need to do is supply her with the materials she needs to make a nice home for her babies."

"What kind of materials does she need, Caroline?" Mom asks.

I can already hear Dad complaining about more things to buy for the rabbit.

"She needs a small box or crate that she can get in to— to feed the babies but that the babies also can't climb out of. She'll also need some hay, like timothy hay, to line the bottom of it. You don't have to buy an expensive crate. You can make one out of wood if you like."

Dr. Fanning goes to her shelf and grabs some pamphlets.

"Here, take these." She hands them to Mom. "They will give you lots of information to help you get ready. One of them shows you how to build a place for the babies."

"Thanks, Caroline." Mom stuffs the pamphlets in her purse.

"And don't forget to make sure Obeena has plenty of water, fresh vegetables and alfalfa to keep her healthy while she's getting ready for the bunnies to come," Dr. Fanning says as we are leaving.

Back out in the waiting area, Tina pats a chocolate lab while we wait for Mom to pay the lady at the front desk. I watch the lab wag its tail as Tina strokes his back. The owner tells us that the dog's name is Frenchie. He tells Frenchie to give a paw. Tina holds her hand out. Frenchie raises his paw and plops it into Tina's hand. We both smile. I stick my hand out next and Frenchie puts his paw into mine. He's a smart dog.

"Okay, let's go, girls." Mom picks up the carrier. We say goodbye to Frenchie and follow Mom out the door.

Tina and I are excited, but I don't want to show it too much, just in case Mom isn't as happy about it. Now that I know Obeena's not sick, I'll feel better and be able to concentrate on the pledge. Mom isn't talking much on the ride home. I don't think she expected to hear this news from Dr. Fanning. I know I need to tell her about the pledge, but it doesn't seem like the right time.

"What are you going to tell your dad?" Tina whispers.

"The truth," I whisper back.

For the rest of the drive home, I keep imagining how much fun it's going to be to have little bunnies hopping around. I can't wait to tell Patrice.

CHAPTER 21

Let's Tell Everyone

The ride home from the vet seems shorter than the trip there. Mom pulls into Tina's driveway.

"Thank you for letting me come with you to the vet, Mrs. Jefferson." Tina hops out of the back seat and waves goodbye. We smile at each other. I know we'll talk about the bunnies some more later.

"You're welcome, Tina." Mom waves back.

When we pull into our driveway, Mom shuts off the car, but she sits there for a minute.

"Do you know what, Arlaina?"

"No. What?"

"This means that Obeena was already pregnant when Patrice gave her to you."

"Then why wouldn't she tell us?"

"She probably didn't know. That male rabbit she gave to Mrs. Wilson at the end of the street must be the father."

"What do you think Dad will say about all this?" I ask.

"Your father will probably have a fit thinking about all those baby bunnies hopping around."

I laugh. I can see Dad having a fit, then Mom telling him that the bunnies are staying anyway.

"We'll let your father know, but be prepared for the bear to start growling." She laughs.

"You can handle him, Mom." I laugh with her.

When we get inside, Kyle is playing video games in the living room.

"Where's your father?" Mom asks.

"He still hasn't come home from work yet." Kyle looks up at Obeena. "So, what's the verdict? Is the furball okay?"

"Don't ask," Mom says.

"She's pregnant," I blurt out.

Kyle pauses the game and looks at Mom. His mouth is open wide.

"Pregnant!" he screeches. "So we're going to have like a hundred bunnies in the house?"

"A hundred? Really, Kyle?" Mom chuckles.

"You'd better take that bunny and split, Arlaina," Kyle teases. "Dad will never go for it. Get out and hide while you still can! Take the rabbit and run far, far away!" He laughs.

I kick him in the leg. He grabs his knee and pretends to be in pain.

"Listen, having bunnies in the house is not the end of the world," Mom says "So let's try not to make such a big deal about it for now, okay? Arlaina, take the rabbit upstairs."

Mom gives me the pamphlets from her purse. I take Obeena out of the grey carrier and take her upstairs to the cage. Now that she's pregnant, I try to be extra careful. As soon as I set her inside, she hops away and wraps her tiny mouth around the tip of the water bottle. As I'm watching her, I hear Dad's truck pull up. I hope he lets me keep the bunnies.

"Dad's here!" I can hear Kyle calling through the house.

"Honey, you're home," I hear Mom say. "We have to chat."

"Does it have to be right now? I'm really tired and hungry, and I need a long, hot bath."

It doesn't seem like the right time to be telling him about the bunnies. I cross my fingers and hope Mom waits until tomorrow.

"It's kind of important." She keeps pressing.

"Anita, do you know that Cameron down at the woodworking plant screwed up our new system and set off some alarm in the building? We had to stop production and figure out how to get the alarm unstuck. We had two hundred orders that were supposed to go out before the end of the day. Guess how much money Cameron's recklessness cost us today?"

Let it go, Mom. He clearly wants to relax.

"Okay, how about I fix you something to eat and run you a bath? Then we can talk afterwards."

"Whatever it is, how about we chat in the morning instead?"

"Okay," Mom agrees.

I'm glad. But until Mom lets Dad know about Obeena, I don't want to add more grief by talking to them about the pledge. I stick my hand in the cage and rub Obeena's fur. She moves away from me and I take my hand back out. She stretches out on her side. I imagine a bunch of little bunnies moving around inside her belly. It seems like that would hurt, but Obeena looks really comfortable. Now that I know she is going to be a mom, I think she looks different. I close the cage and spread the pamphlets across my bed. I want to read everything I can about this bunny box.

The phone rings and I hear Mom talking to Patrice, telling her about Obeena having babies. Then she calls up to me to pick up the line. Patrice can't speak to me for too long, but she is very excited and tells me to let her know everything that happens with Obeena. Before she goes, she lets me read my speech to her. When I'm finished, she pauses for a minute, then gives her advice.

"If you're going to do this, you have to go all the way," she says.

"What do you mean?"

"Your words really have to make the teachers feel something. Let me suggest a few things."

I grab my pen and start writing. When we say good-night, I hang up the phone with a smile. Pledge day is going to be amazing.

CHAPTER 22

Your Pledge Is Your Promise

Nadia is standing in front of the office when Tina and I get to school. Mr. Warren asked all of us to come by so he can make sure we are prepared for the assembly and the pledge.

"Ready?" she asks.

"Yup."

We slip inside the door. The secretary waves us into Mr. Warren's office in the corner. Not long after we get there, Chris and the others pop their heads in.

"Not much space, boys, but come on in. Leave the seats for the young ladies, though." Mr. Warren smiles at them.

Nadia, Tina and I slide into the only chairs in the office. The boys stand around behind us. I would be fine standing up, but maybe Mr. Warren is teaching the boys to be polite.

"I'm glad you all came on time. I am anxious to hear from you. This is very important, what you are trying to do. I must say, you've opened my eyes to some things that I didn't know were issues in this school."

I think again about Kyle saying the pledge is a bad idea. Mr. Warren makes it sound so serious and important. Now I feel like this is going to be huge. I'm glad Kyle was wrong.

"So this is your chance to enlighten me about your experiences here. Who wants to start?"

I feel confident now and I raise my hand.

"I think Mr. Matthews has a real problem with me." I sit up straight in the chair. I'm finally getting my chance to say how I've been feeling about him. "Not I *think*, but I *know* he has a problem. He always makes comments to me. He never believes what I say. He is rude. He has said things about my hair."

"What kinds of things about your hair?" Mr. Warren rubs his chin.

"If my hair is open, like in an afro and not in braids

or ponytails, then he will make a comment about it being too puffy. I never hear him say anything about the other kids' hair."

"He's made comments to me about how I cover my hair," Nadia adds. "He pretends he wants to know about my culture, but the way he says stuff . . . it's like he wants you to feel like you're different."

Mr. Warren's forehead wrinkles more and more as we all speak. It isn't just complaints about Mr. Matthews; some of the kids have stories about other teachers. There are things happening that even I didn't know about. We talk about how we learn Canadian history in class, but none of it includes the history of Indigenous people, or Black people like us. We tell Mr. Warren that we want teachers to understand how their actions make us feel. Mr. Warren says he is happy we came to him and tells us there must be a change. After we leave his office, we feel so much better.

"Gosh, that was like taking off all those heavy winter clothes when the spring comes," Chris says. "When everything seems new."

We all agree. We can't wait for the assembly tomorrow.

After a nervous sleep, the assembly is finally here. I'm still feeling good about our talk in Mr. Warren's office yesterday. Nadia is already standing beside my desk waiting when Tina and I get to class. She looks amazing in her floral blouse and jeans. Her headscarf is a pretty pastel blue. We must have been thinking the same because I also put on one of my best floral blouses and new jeans. We want to look our best when we speak at the assembly. Tina is also wearing a pretty peach top with a blue jean skirt.

"Ready, girls?" Nadia is bubbling over.

"Yes. I'm so excited," I answer.

We sit at our desks as Mr. Matthews starts class. He grabs a piece of chalk and writes the date on the board. Just then, Mr. Warren's voice comes over the speaker and instructs the teachers of fourth-, fifth- and sixth-graders to start bringing their classes to the gym.

Mr. Matthews looks like a scolded student. I don't know why he even started writing. Everyone knew the assembly would be starting in first class. I look at Nadia and smile because we know that Mr. Warren has already spoken with the teachers. He made sure they all knew about the pledge. I wish I could have been in the room when Mr. Warren shared our concerns with the teachers. I hope he yelled at Mr. Matthews and made him feel bad.

The students are happy to be getting away from the classroom. As we make our way down the hall toward the gym, we start to mix in with the other classes heading there too. There is a lot of chatter as we pile into the gym. Nadia motions for the boys to come toward us. We have a little huddle in a back corner. Nadia gives everyone a little pep talk.

"Okay, my friends, today is our day. Don't be nervous,

okay? We know what we have to do. This is important. Arlaina, do you know what you're going to say?"

I nod my head. We all scuffle around to find seats. Soon, Mr. Warren comes through the crowd and taps those of us whose names were on the paper Nadia gave him. I thought he would do the pledge last, but I was wrong. The seven of us follow Mr. Warren to the front of the stage. We stand off to the side while he goes over to the podium and adjusts the microphone. Once everyone is seated in their chairs, Mr. Warren clears his throat and the gym goes silent.

"Thank you, boys and girls, for getting seated so quickly. I know everyone is waiting to hear from the presenters about the summer camp. I know many of you can't wait to sign up for hiking and horseback riding. But I have asked the speakers to come just a little bit later so that we as a school can have a few moments to take care of something that probably should have happened a long time ago. It was brought to my attention by the students you see standing up here that we as a school have not been doing everything we can to make sure everyone feels like they belong. And we need to make that right."

Nadia grabs on to my hand. I squeeze hers as Mr. Warren explains the idea of the teacher's pledge. Then he calls the teachers to the front.

"I want all of my teachers to think about three questions. These are questions that the students behind me want to ask you. Then a few of them will come to the microphone to share what's on their mind."

I look over and see Mr. Matthews standing there looking awkward.

"Question one: Have you ever made a comment to one
of your students related to their appearance? Question two:
Have you ever made a comment to one of your students
based on their race or ethnicity? And last question: Have
you ever made a comment to one of your students that
might have made them feel unequal or less than their peers?
Maybe you've never thought about any of these things
before, or what it meant for the student on the other end
of your words. Or how your comments may have still been
affecting your student long after you've said them. But now,
think about all of these things as you listen to some of these
students speak."

Mr. Warren motions for Nadia to come to the microphone. She slips her hand out of mine. Mr. Warren lowers
the microphone stand for her. Nadia pulls a piece of paper
from her pocket and lays it on the podium. Her voice is
strong. She is not scared.

"Good morning. I am happy to have this chance to
talk to everyone. Some of us here are a little shyer, so only
Arlaina and I will speak. But we speak for all of us up here.
We also speak for other students in the school who feel
like we do. I have not been a student here for very long,
but in this short time, I have been made to feel different.
Because of my colour. Because I wrap my hair. Because
I am from Egypt. But I am no different than any other
student. I was asked about my headscarf in class. But not

because my teacher wanted to know about my culture, but because he tried to show me that I was different. And that is not okay. I want all the students to know that we are more the same than different. I like lunchtime and math problems and nice jeans. I hate brussels sprouts and snakes and cold weather. We just want all of the teachers to know that they have to help bring us together. They have to be a part of the solution and not part of the problem. Thank you."

Everybody claps as Nadia steps away from the microphone. She spoke really well. I think her parents probably helped with her speech. I am happy Patrice helped me add some good stuff to mine. Tina nudges me when it's my turn.

"You can do it," she whispers as I walk over to the microphone.

I pull out my piece of paper and press it out on the podium. I am nervous, and my hands shake. Then I hear Patrice's voice in my head saying I have to speak with power.

"Hi, everyone." I hope my voice doesn't sound nervous. I try to speak loudly. "I watched a protest on television not that long ago. And the people were protesting because of what happened to a boy named Dillan Gray. My dad said they were standing up for what they knew wasn't right. But they were doing it in a way that was peaceful and meaningful. And that's what we're trying to do today. We believe it's not right that we don't learn about the beauty of the many countries in Africa. So kids think the entire continent is a dump and that all the Black kids should go back to it."

I pause, remembering that day in the hallway with Jonathan. I catch his eye in the front row and he looks ashamed. Standing up tall, I continue reading.

"We think it's unfair that we're not taught how this land belonged to First Nations people before it was even called Canada. And how their land was taken from them by settlers. If we learned these things, some of the white kids who think their families made Canada will come to know the difference. And that if *we* should go back to Africa, then *they* should go back to wherever their ancestors came from, too, and give all this land back to First Nations people." I look over at Robbie and Silas. They both smile at me. Before I look back at my paper, I turn my head to the teachers and notice Mr. Matthews shifting from one foot to the other. His arms are crossed—but not like they were when I was doing my presentation in class. This time, his arms are wrapped tightly across his chest. He looks like he's guilty of something. I smile again and keep reading.

"But we all want to make Canada our home. So Black, white, Indigenous, Asian, Muslim, Jewish, everybody—we have to learn how to live together. Instead of that negative stuff, our teachers should be sharing this true history with us, so we can learn to understand each other better. We hope this pledge will be our teachers' promise to help us make this change. Thank you."

I feel proud of myself when everyone claps. I also feel the back of my neck get hot. Maybe it was hot the whole

time, but I didn't notice until I was finished. I grab up my paper as Mr. Warren comes back to the microphone.

"And now I want to read this pledge. This is our pledge as leaders in this school that we make to our students today and going forward. And as each teacher signs it, you are vowing to do your part to make this school a better environment for everyone."

The clapping from all the students sounds like thunder. By now, Mr. Matthews is also clapping. I think our speeches moved him.

"The teacher's pledge goes like this: As an educator in our school, I promise to do my part to make sure it is an equal, fair and safe space for all students—no matter who they are, what they look like, where they were born or what they believe. I further promise to support our students of colour, whose voices may not have been heard, and to correct others when I see a wrong being done to anyone. Lastly, I promise to provide opportunities for in-class discussions, so that *all* students can learn about the beauty of other cultures, countries and people."

I smile. Mr. Warren did a great job of helping us perfect the pledge with those powerful words. When he finishes, the students clap again as the teachers sign the pledge one by one. Nadia's hand squeezes mine again. Tina is grinning wide. None of us can take the smiles off our faces, and I don't want to. This is one of the happiest days I've ever had at Grover Public School. Now that it's a success, I can't wait to tell Mom and Dad—and Kyle—what we did.

CHAPTER 23

Family Matters

The dinner table is buzzing at my house. Everybody has stories they want to share. Kyle wants to talk about the trip we'll be taking to New York when school is out. He is trying to make Mom and Dad pick a date. I sure hope they pick one soon. I know the trip will be amazing. Dad is rambling about something Cameron did at work. I'm dying to tell everyone about the teacher's pledge, but I can't get a word in through all the loud chatting. And Mom still hasn't told Dad that Obeena is pregnant. But I'm sure she will try and bring it up. Finally, Mom sticks her fingers in her mouth and whistles. It makes us jump, but everybody stops talking right away.

"Okay, okay! What is all of this extra thrill at the table tonight? I want to hear what everyone has to say, but can we just talk one at a time? You guys are going to give me a headache," she says.

"Me first, then?" Dad raises his hand like he's in school. Kyle and I laugh.

"Okay, go," Mom says.

"I was trying to say that I was called into the head office today. The lead supervisor is retiring, and I was offered his job. I'm finally going to be able to install that pool out back you kids have been begging for."

I clap and say, "Yay! We're getting the pool! Hello, summer!" Kyle jumps up from the table, does a little dance and sits back down.

"That's my good news. Who else?" Dad smiles.

Mom looks at me. She's about to break the news.

"I'll go next," she says. "So, Arlaina and I took the rabbit to the vet the other day. Do you recall that?"

"Sure." Dad nods and sips from his glass.

"Well, the vet told us that Obeena's going to have a batch of bunnies soon."

"Huh?" Dad chokes on his water.

"Ha-ha! A hundred little bunnies running all around the house. How do you like that, Dad?" Kyle taunts. He's making things worse by laughing.

I wait for Dad to scream and tell me that Obeena has to leave, and that he will take her to live with the grouchy lady down the street.

"Well." Dad rubs his chin as he thinks. "Looks like we're going to have to start building. The bunnies are going to need some place warm to sleep."

We all look at each other in shock. Is this my dad or is it someone else inside his body?

"Honey, are you sure? At first you didn't even want Obeena here," Mom says.

"I had my reasons for that," he answers. "Did I ever tell you about the time I owned a rabbit?"

"No." I shake my head.

"I was about ten years old, and I was being really irresponsible when it came to my rabbit. I named him Dash because he hopped around so fast. I never listened to my mom when she told me to look after him. One day, I didn't shut his cage all the way and he got out. He eventually found his way out the screen door, which I had also left open to go play with my friends. Dash got away and we never found him."

"Oh, that's so sad," Kyle says.

"Yeah, it was. I felt really bad. So I probably overreacted a little when your mom told me you wanted to take this rabbit. But I see that you're not like me, Arlaina. I know you have been trying to take good care of your rabbit."

"And the bunnies?" I have to make sure he is saying yes to the bunnies too.

"*And* the bunnies." He smiles. "But we will have to decide later what to do with all of them. I'm sure when the bunnies are old enough to leave their mother, some of your friends would be happy to have one."

"I think that's a good idea." Mom grins.

"I do too. I'll tell my friends. And if their parents say yes, they can come and pick one out!"

"It's settled, then. We'll work on building them a home." Mom grins.

"I have some more news!" I shout.

"More?" Mom asks.

"Yes. The teacher's pledge!"

"What's the teacher's pledge?" Mom asks.

"Some hairbrained idea she and Tina cooked up," Kyle says. I roll my eyes. Not even he can spoil my excitement.

I explain to everyone how it all started. How we all met at the picnic table and wrote out a pledge. How Mr. Warren helped us make it stronger. I tell them about our speeches in front of the assembly and how Patrice helped me write mine. Mom and Dad's eyes light up as I'm talking. Even Kyle looks surprised.

"That's huge," Dad says. "Why are we only now hearing about this?"

"I wasn't sure if I should say anything or not. I thought you might tell me not to do it. And Kyle said it was like an uprising."

"Since when did you start listening to your brother?" Mom asked.

"Child"—Dad held his hand out for mine—"I don't know why you felt like you couldn't tell us, but don't you remember me telling you about the Million Man March?"

"Yes. That's part of where I got the idea."

"Then I would have loved for you to share that plan with me."

"Sorry, Dad."

"No, don't be sorry. It sounds like it went well. I wish I had come up with something like that when I was your age." Dad looks around the table and smiles. "Wow. Did you all hear what my little girl did? I am so proud of you, Arlaina."

Mom tilts her head toward me and smiles. She looks proud too.

"Okay, okay, so your plan worked," Kyle says. "Good job, little sis. I was wrong!"

I had never heard Kyle say he was wrong before. His words were like music singing in my ears.

"Now, what about my turn!" Kyle squawks. "Can we talk about our trip to New York now, please?"

"Okay, Kyle. It's your turn." Mom laughs.

Dad squeezes my shoulder and winks at me. I feel amazing.

CHAPTER 24

The Builders

"Get up, Arlaina. I have a thought." Mom pulls the blankets off me. I was feeling tired when I came home from school today, so I went straight upstairs after school to have a nap. I wonder why she won't let me sleep. I try to pull the blankets back, but she grabs them all the way off the bed and tosses them on the floor.

"I'm sleepy."

"No way, it's the middle of the day. Since when do you come home from school and take a nap?"

"I stayed up late last night watching Obeena. Tell me the idea first, then I'll decide if I'm going to get up."

Mom laughs. "Oh, you will love this idea. Come meet me in the backyard."

Mom disappears from my room. Now I'm curious. I imagine it's garden work. Every time she needs me to help clean up the backyard or dig in the garden, she traps me into going outside with some kind of pretend plan.

I am only in my underwear and T-shirt, so I climb off the bed and put my grey jogging pants back on. I slip my feet into my black flip-flops and use the bathroom.

"Hurry up!" I can hear Mom's voice ringing all the way up to the bathroom window.

"I'm coming!" I call back.

When I get out back, Mom, Dad and Kyle are standing around a pile of wood. I see a bunch of wire, hammers and some other equipment spread out in the yard. My eyes get big.

"What? Wow!" I squeal.

"This, my child, is everything we need to build a proper home for Obeena and her babies!" Mom shouts excitedly.

At first, I'm just frozen, staring at all this stuff.

"Well, don't stand there looking, it's time to get to work," Dad says. He gets down on his knees and motions for Kyle to join him. Kyle doesn't look excited, but I'm glad to see him helping.

"Do you want to help us build this thing or not?" Mom smiles.

"Yes! Yes!" I clap and rush over to the long, rectangular pieces of wood.

Dad explains that the house will be outside, but Obeena and her bunnies will have shade and protection from any rain and bad weather. He hammers four long stakes into the ground.

"Even though the backyard is fenced in, we still need to make sure the cage will be up high enough in case a stray dog finds its way into the yard," Dad explains.

Following Dad's instructions, Mom and I lay out the wood to wrap the wire fence around it. That will form the outside of the cage.

"On the inside, we will make it so that after Obeena has her babies, she can be on one end and the bunnies can be on the other."

"So why can't they all be together?" Kyle asks.

Mom explains that mother rabbits don't lie with their babies like cats do. She says that mother rabbits feed their babies and then leave them alone in their nest until the next feeding. She must have read all those pamphlets from Dr. Fanning.

As we all get into the work, Mom and I are having a hard time trying to build the base strong enough to hold the wire cage.

"All hands on deck!" Dad orders. He and Kyle jump in and help us with it. Dad sturdies the wood by drilling in more screws while the rest of us hold the structure in place. Then he and Kyle wrap more wire and secure it to the base. We clap when it's finally strong enough to hold.

After a few hours of working on Obeena's house, we are finally finished. The house is big, and it looks good. If I was a rabbit, I would love it. Kyle complains about how hard it was to put it together. I don't care how hard it was, I'm just happy it's done. It makes the arrival of the bunnies even more exciting.

"Thank goodness this torture is over," Kyle grumbles.

"Don't be so negative, son. Your work is just beginning."

Dad laughs. "I'll be expecting you to help your sister with the care and upkeep of all those rabbits."

Kyle puts his hands on his hips and sighs. I laugh because I know he will have no choice but to help me.

"Not too boring, now, is she?" I keep laughing. Kyle is annoyed at me, but I like the payback.

CHAPTER 25

Obeena and Her Babies

At school, Nadia, Tina and I are sitting on the picnic table, rambling about the teacher's pledge. I run inside quickly to use the bathroom. On my way back out, I pass by Mr. Matthews.

"Oh! Arlaina," he calls back to me. I wonder if I should keep walking and pretend not to hear him.

"About the pledge," he says. I turn around to face him. Now I want to hear what he has to say.

"You did a good thing for . . . well, you know, for the kids in the school like you."

"Like me?"

"Yes, the kids who felt unheard. You did a good thing. I hope you feel heard now." He flashes a thumbs-up.

"Thanks."

I walk back outside toward the picnic table. I hope when we're gone to middle school, his actions at Grover back up his sort-of apology.

I tell Nadia and Tina about my encounter when I get to the bench.

"The pledge even changed Mr. Matthews." Tina claps.

"Hmm . . ." Nadia rubs her chin. "I hope so."

Chris and his two friends stop by the bench. "Hey, Arlaina, are all your bunnies spoken for yet?" Chris asks.

"I don't know how many she's going to have yet, but if there's enough, do you want one too?"

"Yeah. I already asked my parents and they said yes."

"Okay, cool."

"Can we see them being born?" He lights up.

"Sure, you can come. If you give me your phone number, I'll call you when it's happening. Nadia and Tina are coming, and a few other kids."

"It's going to be a party." Tina giggles.

"It will be exciting for sure," Nadia adds.

"What if she has them when we're sleeping?" Chris asks.

"I hope that doesn't happen," I answer.

"Okay, I'll give you my number when we get back in class after lunch. Make sure you call me when it goes down. Me and the guys will come over to watch." Chris and his friends take off toward the basketball net.

"Okay, change the subject back for a minute." Nadia gets serious. "Do you think Mr. Matthews is different?"

"It seems like in class he thinks about what he's going to say now before he says it," I answer.

"He hasn't made any more comments about your hair, Arlaina," Tina adds.

"Or about my headscarf," Nadia says. "But did he seem honest when you bumped into him in the hall?"

"I think so. I feel like he will continue to follow the pledge." I smile.

The last day of school is just for an hour so we can pick up our report cards and say goodbye to our friends. I walk out of the front doors of the school with Nadia and Tina. It will be our last time to ever walk the school grounds as Grover students.

We will really miss the picnic table, but we're happy to be moving on to middle school and grade seven. I see Mom pulling up to the school as we are walking out. It's strange because Mom hardly ever drives to the school unless it's important. When she gets out of her car, I can see the panic on her face.

"Let's go, Arlaina! Obeena is going to have the bunnies soon!" she calls out. The students standing around heard what she said. Everybody gets excited.

"Can we ride with your mom?" Tina asks.

"Yeah, come on."

"We're coming too, Arlaina," one kid calls out. A bunch of them start running down the sidewalk to get to my house. They wave to us as we pass by them in the car.

"Are all those students coming to watch Obeena have her bunnies?" Mom asks.

"Yes, it's a party!" Tina squeals.

"Oh my." Mom sighs.

When we get in the house, we rush right up the stairs. I notice a few drops of blood on some of the shavings in Obeena's cage. There is also some blood in the little box we'd made the day we came home from the vet. Earlier, we had taken the fur Obeena pulled out and placed it in the little box with some hay, like the vet told us to.

Mom sees the look on my squished-up face.

"The pamphlet says a little blood is normal when a rabbit is just about to give birth," she assures me. "When I saw it, I figured I would come and pick you up with the car so you wouldn't miss anything."

"Good. Thanks, Mom."

We keep checking on Obeena to see if she's about to have the bunnies. But each time we check, there is nothing happening. Dad is still at work and Mom is on the phone, letting Patrice know what's going on. Soon, the kids from school start arriving. My bedroom is getting packed with students. Kyle walks in from his school and peeks into my room. His eyes pop open when he sees all the kids.

"Whoa," he says.

"Obeena's about to have her bunnies soon," I announce to him.

"There's too much breathing going on in here. Let me know when it's done. I'm going to go play my video game," he says.

"Does anyone want a snack?" Mom calls from the bottom of the stairs.

Almost everybody in the room calls back, "Yes!"

Some of the kids are sitting around the cage beside me. Others are standing around, and a bunch more are crowded on my bed. We're all waiting for something to happen. Tina is right, it is like a party. But instead of music, we will have a birth.

"Your rabbit looks really uncomfortable," Chris says, sitting beside me.

"She's about to have a whack of bunnies popping out of her body. Of course she's uncomfortable," Nadia says.

"Will this be gross?" another kid asks.

"Yes," Nadia answers.

We all laugh.

Mom appears in the room with juice boxes and a tray full of snacks. Everyone stops paying attention to Obeena for a minute and starts digging in for treats. I'm way too nervous to eat. Mom steps over by the cage and watches. She's studying Obeena closely.

"Oh! Oh! Look, look! It's happening now, everyone. The bunnies are coming!" Mom screeches.

Everyone rushes to the cage. We all watch in silent amazement as Obeena shifts her body from side to side. I think I can hear tiny little moans, but no one else is saying they hear them, so I don't mention it. Maybe it's someone chewing on a snack. Finally, we see the first little bunny come out. Everybody starts screaming and squealing. We haven't seen anything like it before.

"Shh!" Mom says. "You must stay quiet, so you won't scare the rabbit."

We try to stay silent as the other ones come out but it's super hard. We are all stunned watching this. Kyle hears the commotion and pushes his way to the front of the cage. Mom looks up at him.

"There they are, Kyle. Six tiny bunnies all curled up together inside the little box."

Obeena is lying there looking up at us. Kyle looks into the cage.

"But they're black," he says. "And they don't have any fur."

"That's normal, Kyle," Mom explains. "These bunnies will start to grow their fur after a couple of weeks."

Now I'm sure Mom read all those pamphlets.

"How long do we have to wait until we can put them in the big wire cage we built in the back-yard?" I ask her.

"Not until they have their fur and are hopping around a bit, at least," Mom says.

"Wow. I guess that's pretty cool," Kyle says. He sits down next to the cage and stares at Obeena's babies.

Everybody wants one of

the bunnies. I tell them I have to give them to the first six people who asked. Two of them were Tina and Chris. Nadia wants to visit them, but she doesn't want one for a pet. After we all calm down from the excitement, everybody finishes their snacks. Now I'm hungry. I munch on some cheese and crackers. Eventually, the kids start leaving to go home. When it's just me and Tina left, we sit around the cage staring at the new bunnies.

When Dad gets home, Mom tells him about the birth. He pops into my room to look at the bunnies. Kyle is right behind him. Dad smiles when he sees them.

"Well done, Arlaina. There's not a hundred like Kyle said there would be, but that's a good thing, right, Kyle?"

We all laugh. Kyle pretends to ignore us.

CHAPTER 26

The Heart Stuff

It's been a few weeks since Obeena had the bunnies. They have started to grow their fur, and now they look like real fluffy baby bunnies. Three of them are brown, like Obeena. The other three have darker fur. Now that it's summer vacation, I can be with them all the time. The temperature is now really warm. We move Obeena and her bunnies outside to the cage we built. It looks very cozy and Obeena seems to be okay with it. Of course, I call Patrice and tell her. I keep her updated on everything that's happening with Obeena and her bunnies, and she's always so excited.

The bunnies are busy all the time, hopping around each other. At nighttime, they all curl up together to sleep. Tina comes over every day to hang out. We hold the bunnies, cuddle them and keep them company. They are way too cute. I feel like they each have a different personality. I know the kids who take them will make up their own names for the bunnies, but Tina and I give them some names anyway. It's so we can tell which one is which. We named the tiniest one Minnie. The one that speeds around the cage we named Bullet. We call the three bunnies with the darkest fur Cocoa, Brownie and Mocha. And we name the only boy bunny Puff, because he looks like a puffy ball of fur.

I'm learning so much from caring for Obeena and all her bunnies. I like when the kids from school drop by to visit them. I like to show them off. I'll be sad when it's finally time for them to go with their new owners, but I will still have Obeena.

When me and Kyle leave for our visit to New York, Mom and Dad take care of the bunnies for me. Aunt Dottie, Uncle Gus and Patrice pick us up at the airport. As we drive through the city, it looks like everything I saw in my dreams. The city is full of noise and full of busy people. Everybody has somewhere to go and something to do. Even the shops are amazing. Patrice's parents take us shopping almost every day. We don't always buy things; we just love going to look.

At times I think I will break my neck looking way up to the top of the buildings. They all seem to stretch into the clouds. I brought some pictures of the bunnies with Obeena. Patrice is so happy when I give them to her. She tapes them to her bedroom wall. On our last night there, Aunt Dottie takes me, Kyle and Patrice to see *The Lion King* on stage. It's incredible. The man playing the lion king has a voice that roars like thunder. All of the singers are so great. We sing along as their voices bounce off the high walls. The beating of the drums is so loud it feels like my heart is beating right out of my chest. When we get back to Patrice's house, we still can't stop talking about it. I dream about it the whole night. The next day, when it's time to say goodbye, Patrice and I cry at the airport. We always cry when we have to leave each other.

The week in New York goes by way too fast, but I'm happy to be back home to Obeena and the bunnies. Not long after we get in the house, Tina calls. I've barely emptied my suitcase.

"Hi, Arlaina. I'm so glad you're back. I missed you."

"We just got home, Tina."

"Come on over to my house. You can tell me all about New York and I can tell you my big news."

"Why don't you come over here? While we were away, Dad installed that pool me and Kyle kept begging for."

"Yes, finally! Okay, I'll be right over!"

When Tina gets here, we go to the backyard and sit on the lawn chairs by the pool. I think she'll want to know all about my trip, but instead, she drops news out of nowhere—she likes a guy named Evan.

"Where did you meet this guy?" I ask.

"At the community centre while you were in New York."

"I thought you didn't like going there."

"I don't but you were gone, and Nadia's family is in Egypt for a month. Plus, there's nowhere else to swim."

"Now there is." I grin, pointing to the new pool

"Do you want to meet him?"

"I guess."

Tina calls me as soon as the sun rises. I reach for the phone on the nightstand. My eyes are still closed.

"Hello?"

"It's Tina."

"Hi, Tina."

"I'm going to bring Evan for you to meet today. Will your parents mind?"

"No, I'll just tell them some friends are coming to see the bunnies. But don't come right at lunchtime. I want to sleep until at least eleven."

"Okay, sleepyhead."

I feel like only two minutes went by and it's already eleven thirty. I crawl out of bed. I know Tina will be ringing the doorbell soon. After I get dressed, I go downstairs to grab a bowl of cereal. Dad has gone to work, and Mom is working out in the living room. I peek my head in to tell her about Tina coming. She nods in between a stretch.

Tina shows up at my back door. Two boys with curly dark hair are standing with her. I squish up my nose and give her a look.

"Follow me." I motion with my hand.

We step out to the backyard and I sit on one of the lawn chairs. The three of them sit too.

"This is my best friend, Arlaina."

The boys look at me and smile.

"This is Evan, and this is his cousin, Donny." Tina grins.

The boys are cute, but they really look alike. Same hair, same pasty-white legs sticking out beneath their shorts.

"Hi." Evan nods his head.

"Nice to meet you," Donny says.

"Donny is from Montreal. His family is here visiting," Tina adds.

"Okay," I respond. We don't say much. No one gets in the pool. It's awkward. I don't know why Tina brought them.

Eventually, they all start coming over every day. We do get in the water. I'm not as strong at swimming as I wish I could be, but I love being in the water. Sometimes we clash with Kyle and his friends, who seem to always hog the pool. But we just try to ignore them and swim anyway.

As the time gets closer to the end of summer, I feel like I improved my back stroke. But the ending of summer also gets me thinking about middle school. Everything will be different there. I wonder if I'm ready for it. On one of our last days at the pool, we spent all day swimming, drinking lemonade and eating Dad's barbeque feast. As Tina, Evan and Donny get ready to leave, I hug Tina.

"Three more sleeps before school starts." I giggle nervously.

"I know. I'm so excited."

I say goodbye to Evan and Donny.

"You're pretty," Donny says. It comes out of nowhere. Even he looks shocked by his words.

"Thanks." I smile, but all I can think about is how close Tina and I are to becoming real middle-schoolers.

CHAPTER 27

A New Day

My alarm wakes me up bright and early on our first day of middle school. The summer came in fast, and it was over just as quickly. But I am excited to see what it's going to be like at the new school. I hop out of bed and into the shower. I spend a lot of extra time doing my hair. It has to look perfect. I take the thick braids out and separate the pieces of hair to make waves. Then I spray the waves with sheen. For the first time, I put on some mascara and plum-coloured lipstick. I look in the mirror and pucker my lips. I notice Mom standing behind me and I turn to look at her.

"Wow." She smiles. "My baby is starting middle school."

"I'm not a baby, Mom." I smile back to show off my lipstick.

"I know. You look beautiful." Mom comes closer and wraps her soft hand around my chin. I look up at her. "I'm thinking it's time to have that conversation about getting you a cell phone."

I squeeze my arms around her waist and squeal really loud. She hugs me back and chuckles. My morning is off to a great start.

I meet up with Tina and Nadia, and we walk to school together. Nadia tells us more about her trip back home to Egypt to visit family. As soon as Tina mentions Evan, Nadia rolls her eyes. She tells us she is annoyed by Evan.

"You only met him a few times," Tina says.

"Boys are just trouble." Nadia shakes her head.

"We're the three musketeers." Tina grins. "Who cares about Evan?"

I can tell Tina is trying not to annoy Nadia. She doesn't mention Evan again as we pick up speed the rest of the way to school.

There are students everywhere when we get to the school grounds. Some are hanging around outside. Others are making their way through the front doors. As soon as we step inside and cruise down the hallway, I feel like we are the smallest kids there. The older kids seem so tall. Many of the girls have already started to fill out with hips and butts. Nadia looks down at herself and then looks at us. We all agree that our bodies are completely flat next to these older girls. Some of the boys even have hair on their faces already. I feel like we just stepped into a high school pretending to be a middle school.

Hundreds of nervous seventh-graders pile into the main

gym with us to find out which homeroom class we will be in. The principal announces that the school has started a new system. Each of us will be matched with another new seventh-grader for the day. She calls it the buddy system. We have to travel from class to class with our buddy. The principal says the idea is to help with some of the scary feelings and to make sure we don't get lost.

The three of us cross our fingers. We hope to be in the same class, or at least that two of us will get to be buddies for the day. As the principal goes down the list, calling out names, we feel lucky about those chances. She has already named quite a few classes, and none of our names were called. I spot Donny on the other side of the gym. He doesn't notice me at first, but I keep staring in his direction and waiting. I watch him look through the crowd. As soon as he looks in my direction, I wave my arm. He smiles when he sees me and waves back. I get a fluttery feeling in my stomach.

"Kimberly Hodges?" the principal calls out. "You will be paired up with Tina Hennigar."

Tina and I look at each other. She frowns after hearing her name called. We won't be buddies today and we probably won't be in the same class. Tina and the Kimberly girl finally move toward their teacher standing near the doorway waiting, as all the last names starting with J have been called and none was Jefferson. There is only one class left to call. That means me and Nadia will be in the same class. We squeeze each other's hand as the principal calls out the buddies in the final class.

"Okay, and last class . . . Arlaina Jefferson, you will be buddies with Duncan Turner . . ."

I gasp out loud. Did she just say Duncan? The bully from Grover Public School? I look around for him. He is standing not far behind me. I look at Tina. She looks as horrified as I feel. I start to walk toward my new homeroom teacher. Duncan comes to my side. He reaches his hand out for me. I just stare at it. Is this a trick? I'm not sure if I should grab his hand or spit on it.

"Truce?" he says.

I can't tell if he means it. I'm still looking at his hand.

"My bad about the field trip last year. And that was real cool . . . that pledge thing you did."

I think back to how the teachers on that field trip automatically believed him and not me. I hope they were all thinking about this Black girl when they were signing the pledge.

Duncan stretches his hand out to me again. I almost don't shake it. Getting me sent to the bus was mean, and I missed out on the biggest trip of the year. Duncan was used to picking on kids like me. I look down at his hand, then I look at his face. I remember what my friends and I fought for by creating that pledge. I remember seeing Duncan's face in the crowd that day, looking like it does right now. He wants me to forgive him. It seems to make sense for me to give him another chance. I reach out and shake his hand. Duncan looks relieved.

I didn't even know he could make his face smile like

that. I only ever saw it look mean. Smiling makes him look like a real person with real feelings.

As the day goes on, I get more surprised by how much I enjoy having Duncan as my buddy. I had no idea he was so funny. We get lost in the gigantic school more than two times. Duncan does some impressions of famous actors. He's pretty good at pretending to be them.

As we chat more, I tell him all about Donny and how I met him. Duncan tells me about a girl he likes named Abby. When we pass by Abby in between classes, Duncan points her out. She is full of freckles and is wearing thick glasses with blue rims. She is as skinny as a French fry with her hair dyed pink. I like her hair. Duncan waves to her. He turns totally red when she smiles and waves back. I want to laugh out loud about his crush because they seem like complete opposites. But I think Duncan might take my laughter the wrong way.

When the school day is over, Nadia, Tina and I meet up at our lockers.

"How did it go?" Tina asks.

"Our homeroom teacher is Muslim, and she wears a headscarf like me." Nadia beams.

"And she's very nice," I add.

"My teacher is a dude. But he seems nice too."

We grab our bags and head down the hall. As we're walking, I look into all the faces that we pass. Some of them are familiar faces from Grover, and others are strangers. I think about all the stories they must have. They probably didn't do the pledge like we did, or watch a rabbit give birth to new bunnies, but I'm sure their stories are just as interesting. I eventually hope to learn some of them.

I also hope the teachers are thinking about all of us as equals. Then me and my friends won't have to stage an uprising at this school too. But if we need to, I know we will have our Grover pledge friends and my dad behind us a hundred percent.

"Here comes your little boyfriend," Nadia teases as Evan comes toward us.

"Can I walk you three pretty girls home?" Evan smiles.

"Why do you ask when you will just do it anyway?" Nadia giggles at him. "I guess you can come along."

Nadia makes sure Evan knows that we girls are the bosses and that we are *letting* him walk with us. Evan is so excited, he trips over his own foot. As we stride past the main office, we are still laughing hard. Evan swings the school's front door wide open, and the four of us all jam through it together, out into the September sunshine.

Acknowledgements

An endless thank-you to Suzanne Sutherland, who plucked this story from the pile and championed it right from the start. Your belief in the journey of these middle-grade characters and the importance of the message has made all the difference. Incredible appreciation and gratitude are extended to Chelene Knight, my amazing agent. Your hard work got us here. Special thanks to Yash Kesanakurthy, whose editorial insight planted seeds and sparked conversation. To all the eyes and hands that touched the manuscript, your commitment to culturally diverse storytelling is evident throughout this book.

PHOTO BY RACHEL McGRATH

WANDA TAYLOR is the author of both fiction and non-fiction books for children and adults. She is a former CBC Television producer and a documentary filmmaker. Wanda is a freelance journalist, screenwriter and college instructor. She also serves as faculty and a mentor in the MFA writing and publishing program at University of King's College in Halifax, Nova Scotia. Her magazine features can be found in numerous publications across North America, and her poems and short stories also appear in collections and anthologies across Canada, the US and the UK. Wanda Taylor teaches courses in journalism, communications and story writing for media.